In **The Road to Matewan**, William Trent Pancoast writes an ode to the land of Appalachia while giving a voice to its marginalized people. With spare but lyrical prose, Pancoast tells the story of Thomas Greene, one man confronted with the destructive forces of modernization and industrialization, and the choices he's forced to make to be free. **The Road to Matewan** is a historical novel that resonates with present-day political relevance, and William Trent Pancoast is an emerging writer to watch.

--**Amy Greene**, author of **Bloodroot** and **Longman**

Pancoast returns to mythic ground in depicting the history of mining in Appalachia and the battle between the agrarian and industrial, but at the heart of this story is Thomas Greene, a man uniquely his own, dedicated to the promises of freedom and a life emanating from the land he loves. Pancoast well knows this sweeping history, easily transporting his reader back to this important time.

--**Denton Loving**, author of **Crimes Against Birds**

The Road to Matewan is a novel of the slow inexorable drag into trouble that is Appalachia's history in the late nineteenth and twentieth century. Told in prose both economical and beautiful, William Trent Pancoast's **The Road to Matewan** is an exquisite short novel about the consequences of that slow drag. As Appalachia goes, so does the country.

--**Rusty Barnes**, author of **Reckoning**

Introduction

William Trent Pancoast

I wrote the first words of this novel in 1972 after taking my grandmother to her childhood home in the Tug Valley of southern West Virginia. When we got back to Charleston, where she had raised her family of three children, she gave me a little paperback book titled Mingo County History. It was in that local history that I first read of the Matewan Massacre. I began immediately imagining her childhood along the Tug River and the history of the Tug Valley, Matewan, and the Battle of Blair Mountain.

There was not a lot of information available about the Tug Valley and the Mine Wars in 1972. Now, mostly published in the last decade, there are many books, fiction and non-fiction, that provide an accurate history of southern West Virginia. For 45 years I have written and rewritten The Road to Matewan. The first draft, finished in 1975, was twice as long as the present version. I persevered because the story of the mountaineers of southern West Virginia was so important and needed to be told to the world.

There will be readers of The Road to Matewan who first encounter this history in my book. Spreading this history is my intent. Appalachia, its coalfields, and especially the Tug Valley, are an American tragedy. When the liars and thieves representing the land and coal companies set about stealing the land from its pioneer owners, no one could have envisioned the feudal state that would be imposed upon the mountaineers of West Virginia. I know how important the history of the Tug Valley is to me, and I have seen how important that history is to the people who were uprooted, and to the descendents of those who stayed. Therefore, The Road to Matewan.

The Road to Matewan

a novel

William Trent Pancoast

Blazing Flowers Press

for Eleanor

Chapter One
1898

Thomas Greene knelt in the garden spot, the soft music of the artesian well in the still dawn a constant soothing, and pulled two clumps of cheat grass from around the base of the bean plants. The bean pods were young and full, a good combination, and today would be the day Gertrude and the kids did the first batch of half runners. Good that the crop had come early as she was due next week with their sixth child.

Beneath the second clump, a piece of iron lay red and crumbling in the manure-rich soil. Thomas plucked it up and held it to the light of the awakening world, the mists holding fast across the river on the Kentucky side, the steepest mountains in the Tug Valley. It was a tine from a cultivator, he guessed, and he pondered the difficulties of living here in this wilderness without the proper tools, a forge-hardened plow blade like he now had, crosscut saws that could cut logs all day, and guns that always fired. His grandfather, or his father as a child, might have left this piece here.

The first ray of the day's sunlight slipped through the topmost leaves of a chestnut tree, and the iron oxide crumbled in flakes as he massaged the reddish piece with his thumb. When all the loose was gone from the iron, Thomas spit on it and continued the massage. The gray and black of iron soon showed itself and Thomas laid the six inch long piece carefully beside a bean plant where he knew one of the kids would find it later. Robert, his oldest son, would make a knife from the piece if he found it.

A tremendous explosion reverberated from over the ridge, the valley channeling the noise and vibration, and Thomas stood. He looked over the western ridge to the mine below where a steam engine belched into action, and he could hear the scraping and clawing of a steel shovel against the heart of the mountain.

Thomas could hear the stirring about in the cabin, and then talking, and knew it was Gertrude and his oldest son Robert. He turned away toward the mountain, and as he picked up the trail a few minutes later on the far side of the hay field, he knew this was a time he needed to be alone. He had stashed his whiskey jug in the cold pool of the spring at the very base of the mountain where it would be out of his wife's sight, and now tilted it to his lips. Even with the chill from the spring the stuff burned his throat and warmed his entire body. He wasn't a big drinker but this day was one of those days that he could feel the darkness covering him, darkness he had felt coming for months.

Even the spring that year, with its renewal of cleansing winds and rains, had not lifted the depression from Thomas Greene. A lethargy, an abstract cancer of the sort that eats on a man's will and pride, had set into him. The excitement that always filled him during his plans for planting was missing.

All along the Tug River were the beginnings of mine camps. The cheap frame houses sprang up in rows along the river and creek hollows where the companies owned the land. Much of the land was flat out stolen by deed manipulation or fake deeds. Much of it also transferred hands through plain old greed: "This land is valuable real estate," the mine and land companies told people. Sell your land, or the mineral rights, and stay right where you are. The company will let you stay while they build the new houses for the camp, and then you can move into a new house and go to work in the mine. And you still have the money that they gave you for your land. Most times, the mountaineers were swindled. Ten dollars for coal, timber, and all mineral rights, and the land and coal men didn't tell you that part of the mine shaft would be on your property, and they took the timber anyways. Five dollars an acre, eight dollars, too many tracts, and the lifeblood of the Tug Valley gone forever.

Thomas had listened to the liars and thieves he had at first been civil to, as they tried to get him to sell his mineral and timber rights and the land itself. A few local mountain men, all with larcenous and murderous histories, were on the payroll of the mine and land companies and Thomas kept his rifle handy when they came around—belligerent, threatening men holding fake deeds granted in

Virginia a hundred years before West Virginia became a state. The worst of these, Devil John Wright, a man reputed to have killed 20 men, sat one day in 1895 in Thomas's cabin waving that fake piece of paper and said he wouldn't go to court if Thomas granted him the mineral and timber rights. Thomas had stood up, face to face with the man, his rifle dangling at his side, and snatched the paper from Wright. Wright reached in his suit breast pocket for his revolver but Thomas had him at the end of his rifle. "I'll kill you if you come here again," Thomas had said. That worked because Wright knew that what he heard was correct—Thomas would have to kill him if he showed up again, to save his land and livelihood, and protect his family.

Thomas had lived through the Hatfield/McCoy feud, his cabin a half hour ride from Devil Anse Hatfield's. A man could be stopped at any time during those years by pickets set up by one side or the other. Once on the road to Matewan, he was mistaken for Wall Hatfield and only escaped only because he was ready with his rifle. Another time he was kidnapped by three members of the McCoy clan, who mistook him for a Hatfield, and taken up the mountain on the Kentucky side of the Tug. The Kentucky men had been drinking all day, and when the sudden darkness and rain caught them drunk and unawares they found shelter in an abandoned cabin. When they got drunker and fell asleep, Thomas cut the ropes, with a McCoy knife, from his hands and ankles, crept away into the thick forest, and made his way home. Folks knew Thomas and knew he could use a gun, the only law there was sometimes in the Tug Valley.

No matter how the forests and farms were acquired by the land and mine corporations, excitement spread through the Tug Valley. Jobs at the mines were coming. A dollar and a half, two dollars a day. Company stores filled with the simple staples that had always been hard to get in these isolated mountains. In a land still in pain from the butchery and hatred of the Civil War and then the Hatfield and McCoy fighting, where cash money was scarce, the coal mines looked like a good deal to many of the mountaineers.

Halfway to the top, Thomas sat on a huge wedge of sandstone and worked on the jug. On the hillside bordering his land, on the land that Thomas's cousin had sold, four large houses were the first to be built. Rows of windows on the second stories faced down on the valley. Huge screened enclosures graced the front porches. A stairway was cut into the hillside and freshly sawed timbers were placed as steps. Along with these mansion-like structures and they were mansions in comparison with the weathered cabins that dotted the hillsides and valleys here and there the company store was built at the base of the mountain and stocked with canned goods and clothing and miners' tools and equipment.

Shortly after these structures on the hillside were finished, their new residents arrived. The engineer, the mine operator, and the other members of the management hierarchy filled these first homes so that they could oversee the layout and construction of the mine and the camp. One of the homes would remain vacant to serve as a guesthouse for the owner for the infrequent trips he would make to his property.

Thomas had watched it all in despair, this industrial affront to his mountains an affront to him so deep he knew it was his soul that was aching. Dawson, the mine operator, employed by Harris Mining, had been over to see him. One thousand dollars, he had told Thomas. One thousand dollars for your land. So confident was the man that he had begun thumbing off the hundred-dollar bills.

"Get off my land," Thomas had told him.

After the company store was completed, Joe Davis, Thomas's uncle, was over to see him. "I never paid no attention to what you said about these companies coming in here. I wish now that you was wrong. But you wasn't. They don't want none of my hogs. I even bought me a new pair of them special hogs they been usin' up north for breeding. The feller runnin' that company store just laughed at me. They got pork over there in barrels and cans. He says folks won't need to be messin' around butchering no hogs."

Below the hillside on the bottom land along the river, away from the large, well-built homes on the hill, and farther downstream on the land that two of Joe Davis's sons-in-law had lost the deeds to, the miners' homes were built. The houses were of simple design, and a dirt or mud street, depending on the weather, separated the two rows of houses.

Potbelly stoves for heating the homes would be available to the miners at the company store, as would cook stoves. And the coal that would provide heating and cooking fuel would be available at wholesale prices.

As the mine camps sprang up along the newly laid rails, to the east of Thomas, and to the west, and up the several spur lines that had been extended up creeks and hollows, they were filled by men and their families. The Harris Company was opening three mines between Thomas's land and Matewan, and a school was constructed between Mine #2 and Mine #3. At the company store, all a man needed to do to get something, be it tools he would need for mining, clothes for his children, or food for his table, was to sign his name or make his mark, and at the end of the month he would have his purchases and the rent for the house deducted from his pay.

Thomas Greene knew that something irreparable had happened to the Tug Valley. He knew deep inside that what had started here, right in front of him, that which had already made enough noise and dirt for eternity, what had poisoned the mountains with avarice and greed, was a large unstoppable force, and that possibly the only solution was to run from it, save his wife and their children by getting them away from this place. But he couldn't easily do that, could not leave this place of mystery and beauty where three generations of Greenes had lived before him. Where would he go, for starters? That's what really stopped him from fleeing with his family. Where could he go in this whole wide world that he would know what to do? How else could he take care of Gertrude and their children? What else was there to do but what he was already doing—plowing and planting and harvesting? Thomas accepted the inevitable blight of the mines, or rather he resigned himself to it. "Maybe it won't be so bad," he told Gertrude one night after a few glasses of hard cider. "We can still feed the kids. We got our land. We got each other."

At Mine #3, as the houses filled up with miners and their families, and before the mine was in operation, the men were set to work felling trees from the land that the Harris Company owned outright or on which it owned the timber and mineral rights. In a matter of weeks, the former Ferrell land had been stripped of its timber except for the trees left standing around the large homes on the hill. Out of these logs, roof supports for the mines were fashioned at the sawmill that Harris Mining had set up. After the ridges above the mine site had been stripped, the workers moved into the valley and began cutting on the Johnson land, and others of the crew worked on the Davis land. While the majority of the men worked at the timber operation, a handful of others, supervised by the mine engineers, worked at digging out the initial entry into the mountain. All day long the steam-powered equipment droned on, and the dynamite charges were set off, the men blasting and clawing and digging their way into the heart of the mountain, and in a few weeks the coal came rattling through the tipple and into the waiting coal cars.

Thomas was at a loss to understand all that was happening. And it was happening so quickly. There was a growing excitement in the hills and valleys as men flocked to the mines to apply for work. People came from far and near to take the valuable jobs, some of them folks who had never seen a mountain or a coal mine. Black folks, Italians, or Germans—whoever could get there—made their way along with the mountaineers to the new camps and traded whatever lives they had before for the comfort of these new homes and the security that a steady income would guarantee them.

Thomas clutched the jug and made his way up the old Cherokee trail through the chestnuts and oaks. He had felled several chestnuts two years ago, and did not look forward to the back-breaking task of splitting and sizing timbers this summer. But he would do it and the new barn would be built that fall.

Out in the valley he could see the growing patch of bare land near the Johnson cabin, where the workers had been cutting timber, and where the unspoiled green of the valley had once presented itself. Off to his right, the coal tipple stood thrusting its ugly snout above the ridge that partially obscured the mine camp. Farther to the right, the bare hillside stretched lifelessly before him, divested of the foliage that had graced it only this spring. Piles of brush and the limbs that could not be used for timbers lay in piles. Below him, the railroad bank lay like a cinder snake along the river, the rails flashing as the morning sun hit them.

When he reached the top, he sat on a decaying log. From his seat he looked to the north, over the forested land that was still inaccessible to the mining companies. Most of the land in the small valley below him was owned by old man Jenkins, a distant cousin. But he would not sell any of his land. Thomas had talked to him about it. "That's the reason the deed for this land is still in my name," he had told Thomas. "So none of my kin will sell it. I'll never sell, not to nobody."

The tension that Thomas had allowed to accumulate during these last few years, when he was forced to watch something devilish and foul creep nearer and nearer until it smothered his beautiful and sacred valley, lay heavy on him. He thought of it constantly, worried over it like a dog with a bone. Was he alone holding out against this "progress" that was invading his valley? No, he knew he wasn't alone. His father-in-law Gabriel and most of his kin would not sell their land. But it didn't eat at Gabriel the way it did at him. "Stop your frettin'," Gabriel continually told him. "There ain't nothing to be done about it. They own their land just like you own yours."

He tilted the whiskey jug and watched the mists on the far side of the mountain swirling and tossing as the sun began its work on them. The lush green before him was comforting. The land. All a man and his family need to live. And the silence and holy mystery of the earth with all its riches. He sat facing this wilderness, occasionally tilting the jug to his lips, savoring the burning punishment to his innards as the whiskey went down. All around him was the sound and movement of life in his beloved mountains. He dozed to this ancient melody.

Gertrude was uncomfortable in the heat of the summer. But she went on with her work. What was happening around her, the mining boom spreading to the very doorstep of the Greene cabin, the influx of strangers, and the continual commotion of the mine excavation, seemed not to affect her. She was too busy caring for her children and carrying on the work of the household and farm to give much attention to these changes. And the coming of the mines did not bother her as they did Thomas. Yet she hoped that he would grow used to it. He and the children were her life—not the land. She was the bearer of life, carrying their child. The living flesh of her family was what was important to her. She had tried to explain this to Thomas, but though he seemed to understand what she was saying and to agree with her, he could never really understand. He had never felt the unborn child in his body, had never felt the expectation of terror and happiness that each birth brought, and a distance had grown between them as the mine had gradually taken shape through the last year and a half.

In the summer kitchen Gertrude was hard at the task of preparing the canning equipment this morning. Robert and his younger brothers and sisters, James, Mary, William, and Violet, were, of course, a tremendous help with the work. Violet, being only three years old, was more trouble to the troop of bean pickers than she was worth, at least according to Robert, the "boss," as he put it.

He had come to Gertrude earlier when they started work. "Violet just gets in the way. She ain't big enough to be helpin'."

"You were little once yourself ... help her, show her how," Gertrude called after him as he hurried back out to the bean picking. He was such a hard worker that he was responsible for a goodly part of their success on this little mountain farm. But there was a sadness about him that made her afraid. He could not accept love from her and Thomas. When she hugged him she could feel his trouble looking for a place to go.

Thomas awoke to more blasting. When he sat up he could hear the chugging of the steam engine. From the position of the sun, Thomas knew he had slept for a couple of hours. He was groggy from the whiskey he so seldom drank, and felt ashamed for running off the way he had. His commitment to his family was larger than this journey of depression and self pity he had embarked upon this morning. He was a strong and powerful man of these mountains. He stood, slowly turned a complete 360 degrees, and inhaled the beauty of his mountains through both his brain and his lungs. He knew then that the mountains could possess a man just as his wife and his children possessed him.

Thomas left the jug on the mountain and made his way down the north slope. His thoughts of the intruder to his valley left him. It suddenly didn't seem to matter. He wandered along the creek bed on the valley floor, passing a deserted cabin and overgrown farm that had been deserted by a third or fourth cousin thrown into economic chaos by the Civil War. If not for Thomas's kinfolk, the story might have been the same for his homestead when his father was killed at Gettysburg.

He pushed through the honeysuckle and rhododendrons growing beneath the canopy formed by the chestnuts along the creek and stepped down over the bank. The cool, clear water of the shallow rapids felt good on his tired feet as it soaked through his boots. He walked along the smooth-pebbled bottom for several hundred yards until he reached a deep pool and was forced to climb the bank.

All around him the morning buzzed with life. A Black Racer slithered into the water as he stepped from the creek. Thousands of small white butterflies flitted about. Honey bees buzzed everywhere, landing on Mountain Laurel and Hackberry blossoms. Grasshoppers darted away from the trampled path he was making. He stopped and plucked a handful of raspberries from a bush. The sweet, ripe fruit dissolved in his mouth, and he ground the seeds between his teeth. God's fruit. No man could invent raspberries or the soil that made them possible. A man could only tamper with the world, with the land. Thomas took this for granted. Man was inconsequential in comparison with his Creator and the Creator of the land that made his life possible. Goldfinches and sparrows moved about in the undergrowth before him. A woodchuck reared up on its hind legs and watched him.

Thomas sat down on the bed of a weed patch in a bright glen that stretched fifty yards along the creek. For so long—forever, it seemed to him— he had ignored, had been forced away from seeing, the harmony and beauty of God's world that surrounded him. He had dealt too long with violent and soulless men. The idiocy of the killing by mountain men named Philips and Wright. The Hatfield and McCoy dispute originating out of Civil War mayhem. And now the desecration of the land by the mining and timber companies. All these origins of violence seemed now to Thomas to come from the same source—that ancient forcing of men into bondage and servitude by those who have stolen and cheated and killed for personal gain.

The world at this moment had a freshness and vividness that Thomas had never before experienced. He lay down on the grass that stretched from the narrow creek bottom and followed the outline of the trees to the top of the mountain. A half dozen crows squawked by, traveling the route, the flyway, that only they could know. The sky was cloudless and bright blue. He noticed that as the sky reached to its horizon a whitish haze formed. The sky was bluest directly above him. He lay motionless, looking for the absolute bluest spot in the sky. There must be one little speck, he thought, where it is richest and bluest and most beautiful.

He watched the sky, seeking that bluest and richest spot that led to the heavens. He found it and watched it and felt it, becoming one with the forests and creeks and rivers and mountains, and all of the wonders of color and smell and sound. And gradually, as he lay on the coarse grass, he was cleansed and strengthened by his communion with the earth.

He dozed in and out of consciousness for an hour in this relaxed state, and gradually he felt the energy welling up in him, the energy and strength that had allowed him to forge a life in this solitude of wilderness. His thoughts turned to Gertrude and their children, and he saw suddenly, with the same clarity with which he had witnessed God's world, that he must not let the intruders to his valley and their violent ignorance of the world cloud his vision.

Thomas was up then, and running. He pushed along the creek, the wet leather of his boots collecting the fuzzy residue from the fertile land. He ran on, sweating out the whiskey he had drunk earlier, sweating out the waste he had allowed himself to accumulate as he let thoughts of the intruders poison him. He was free. He would always be free. He ran up the hillside that he had earlier stumbled down, the strength pulsing through his every muscle, propelling him up a trail that a band of native Americans had first forced from the land. Up he went taking great strides, and then he stood at the top, for this moment the man in charge of these mountains. He looked out over his forests and ridges, his creeks and rivers, taking deep breaths of the clean, rich air.

He could hear the chugging of the steam engine again, and could see men swarming around the rail siding and the mine entrance on the hillside. They looked tiny and fragile from here. And he thought how insignificant a man must look to his Creator.

He was free. He had his vision. That was all he needed.

Chapter Two

Beyond the conflicting testimonies of written histories and the unwritten histories that lie accumulated in layers onto the earth, one may be certain of one thing: that life is and was and will be dependent on the land—the supporter of life. Thomas Greene knew what supported his life and the lives of his forebears and children and he had chosen to remain as close as possible to that source of life, the land, and to recognize it as the giver of life. He knew that one day he would take his place in the accumulations of extinguished life that lay beneath him on his land, and he did not fear what he knew.

The coal. Let them dig it, he had come to think. Life was not to be lived in ten or twelve-hour shifts for Thomas Greene. His work was his life, his life his work. There was no difference for him. He knew as he plowed or planted or cultivated or harvested or hunted, or cut a tree for a winter's warmth, that he was taking the materials of life directly from their source. And he was once again at peace.

As the men and machines entered the mountain that summer, and the coal accumulated in the rail cars, Thomas put these scenes from his mind. As the slag heap beside the coal tipple grew, and as debris and waste thrown or spilled from the trains accumulated along the right of way, he was able to keep his peace. He was in an invincible situation, he now believed. As long as this land was his, he need not fear the intruders or allow them to separate him from his land.

The coming of the mines had improved the educational system in the valley. Nearly a hundred children attended the three-room schoolhouse that had been built between Mine #2 and Mine #3. And the state had provided enough money to hire two teachers with degrees. Textbooks were in short supply though, and for the younger children especially, the main text was the Sears and Roebuck catalogue or one of the special-order books from the company stores at the mines. From these the students could increase their awareness of new things. But the clothes, tools, furniture, and other household goods that were displayed throughout the catalogues were alien to many of the children, except those of the management teams at the mines.

Gertrude and Thomas had decided long before the coming of this new school that they would make sure at home that their children were educated. The Bible, newspapers, and the dozen books Thomas and Gertrude had managed to get hold of were read aloud in the evenings, and the children, as they were able, were the readers. William emerged as the lover of books in the

Greene household and by age eight could read anything put in front of him. His favorite was The Adventures of Huckleberry Finn, a book Thomas had traded a large rack of deer antlers for in Matewan.

Robert had decided by the age of twelve that he didn't like school. He continually begged Thomas to let him stay home to help with the work on the farm. "It just don't feel right settin' in there all day while there's work to do," he said. Usually Thomas forced him off to school, but sometimes, when there was a job with which he needed help, he would allow Robert to stay home.

James and Mary, though, came to enjoy their schooling and were continually working on some project or another. And they proved to be more sociable than Robert. He was quieter, had developed a stoic attitude toward people and never wasted speech. He talked only when necessary and worked quickly through any task his teachers gave him. He was always among the first to be finished with any assignment or project at school, and he grew increasingly bored with school life. Through the fall and winter as he sat enclosed within the building, a shot from the forest would bring his imagination into play, and he would wonder if his father or Gabriel or whomever it was had hit his mark. In the spring as the preparation of the land began, he would prowl the schoolrooms ceaselessly, seeking an escape from the cage-like place. There was so much to be done in Robert's view of things—the building and repairing and planting, and witnessing the swift rebirth of the land, all the things he had grown up doing and seeing with his father.

Thomas was strength to Robert, who sought to imitate that strength. And Robert did possess a strength and solidarity unmatched by any of the other Greene children. Of course he was the oldest, and had always been the first to learn to do a job or to help his father with work. He had welcomed the responsibilities that came with his status as firstborn. He was the leader in the work with the other children and knew how to do everything necessary to run the farm. Even with the animals he was proficient. Several times already he had helped with the birth of a foal. And he loved with a passion the work on the farm. Even in the coldest weather he would energetically set about his chores. Robert would rather be outside, facing whatever the world had to offer, than cooped up in the schoolhouse or in the cabin.

When school was through for the year in 1899, the Greene children worked on the farm as in years past. And when their chores were finished each day they were free—free to roam the hills, hike the ancient trails, hunt arrowheads, pick blackberries, go fishing. A wildness overtook the mountain children in the summer. Out of doors from early morning to dark, their spirits were infected with the spirit of the rugged land. Brown and healthy from their adventures in the hills, they were eager for life; they never lacked for anything to do.

Mary and James often played with the mine operator's children. There were three Dawson children—ages five, seven, and nine. They became familiar with the Greene farm and often could be found helping Mary and James with their morning or evening chores. They had never been around a farm or lived in such a place as these mountains, and their time here had been one of eager curiosity and learning about these things that had been withheld from them. They escaped the sooty drudgery of the mine camp whenever possible.

One morning in early August, the Dawson children had been helping James and Mary hoe the vegetable garden. When their work was finished, they set off up the mountain, as was their custom. The youngest Dawson child, David, the five-year-old, had come along with them that morning and had played with Violet for a while. When the older ones started up the mountain trail, David followed. Their plan was to explore the creek beyond the ridge that trailed up away from the Tug and into a lush glen. When they reached the top, the children were eager to get down the steep trail on the other side. Reasoning that David would slow them down, the older Dawson children instructed him to stay at the top.

But an hour had passed when they remembered David and scrambled back up the trail.

David was not where they had left him. They searched the surrounding area, but could not find him. It was afternoon when their search led them to the Greene farm, and the Dawson children finally went home.

Mrs. Dawson alerted her husband at the mine below when she heard about David. He was in his office compiling his monthly expenditures report when she told him. He sat, considering the best course of action.

"Why don't you call the work off early and let some of the men look for him," she suggested.

"I can't do that. We're already behind in production this month. I'll go over to the Greenes'."

"I sent the kids back there already."

"Good. I'll tell the foremen to spread the word to the men. If David's still missing when the shift is over, I'm sure they'll help search for him." He got up and started for the door. "How did he get lost anyway?"

"The kids took him this morning. They were supposed to watch him."

"You let them go off by themselves learning God knows what with these hillbillies around here."

"They like to play. They're just children."

"Damn," he said as he stomped out the door.

Thomas and Robert were sharpening the plow blade before coating it with grease and storing it for the next year's use when Dawson arrived.

"Mr. Greene," Dawson started.

"Still not for sale," Thomas smiled at him.

"No, I don't want … I'm here about my son David. He's lost somewhere in the hills."

Thomas stood up, wiping his hands on his overalls. "I heard the kids talking a little while ago. Said they had to find David. I supposed they were just coming over to your house."

"No. It seems they went up on the mountain this morning and left David on top to wait for them. But he left while they were gone."

"He can't be far. I'll get James to round up some of the folks to help find him if you like."

"I'd appreciate that. I mean …."

Thomas interrupted him. "We'll get all the folks we can to help. If the Davises are willing to help, they can cover the western ridge. Gabriel and the boys and the Hatfields can look to the east. I'll go to the north."

"Thank you," Dawson said. "I'll come with you."

Thomas looked at the man and then down at his feet. "You won't get far in those shoes, and those clothes will get ripped right off you. You got any boots or work clothes?"

"Yes." He looked down at his thin-soled, black leather shoes. "I'll get them and meet you."

"You search behind your house on the other side of the ridge. We'll cover more ground if we stay separate."

Thomas had an idea. Old man Jenkins had the best hounds for miles around. "Track anything," he always said. Thomas sent Robert along with

Dawson. He would get a piece of the lost boy's clothing for the hounds.

In short order a dozen people of the valley had joined the search. Thomas found James and Mary with the Dawson children at the top of the mountain where they had left David. The Dawson girl was crying, but she dried her tears as Thomas gave them instructions. The Greene children would cover the ridge to the east, and the Dawsons would head to the west, where Thomas knew they would meet their father.

When the children had started on their way, Thomas stood for a while surveying the area before him. The hill was steep and rocky directly before where he stood. A child could never have made it down the incline of the trail without falling most of the way. But to the right, on a sort of diagonal line, the slope broadened and would be passable. Thomas chose this line of descent. When he was about halfway down, he found a grassy area where several deer had been bedded. He continued on through a rocky, briar-infested area. It was rough going for him, but a child could easily have walked under the tangle of briars. A rattler slithered off a rock and into a hole.

Thomas pushed on to the creek, carefully measuring the path he took. He scanned both sides of the creek bank, but he could find no sign of the boy. It was only a half mile to the Jenkins cabin, which perched midway up the mountain on the

north side of the valley. The hounds let out an
uproar as Thomas approached. Jenkins came around
the side of the cabin, and when he saw who it was,
he silenced his hounds, kicking one reddish-colored
mongrel which persisted in growling and snapping
at Thomas.

The balding, toothless man approached
them. "Be time to be runnin' coon again if you're
rested up from last year yet," he laughed. Thomas
and Robert had been hunting with the old man the
winter before. They covered miles of territory
whenever they hunted with Jenkins, who prided
himself on his spryness and endurance.

"We're still recovering," Thomas said. "Got
a problem, and I thought you might help us."

"Always glad to help folks.'

"There's a little boy lost out here
somewhere. Only four years old. Lots of folks
hunting for him. We could save ourselves a lot of
time if we could borrow one of your hounds."

"Your boy?" Jenkins asked.

"No. He's Dawson's, the mine operator's."

Jenkins spat sloppily to the side. "If it were
the old man lost, I'd let the hounds tree him and
shoot him out. But little ones. Never seen a bad
little one."

"You'll help, then?"

"These hounds can smell out anything."

Robert had returned and Thomas held out
the shirt he had gotten from the Dawsons. "This
might help."

"Now you're makin' it easy. Yeah. That'll help plenty." Jenkins untied one of his dogs, a black-and-tan female that had been lying quietly under the porch. The other dogs started up their chorus of howls and barks again, jealous that they were not to join the hunt.

"This'n here won't eat the little feller up when she finds him. She's a good tracker but not much for treein'." Jenkins knelt beside the bitch and let her nuzzle and chew the shirt. Thomas led the way down the valley, and as soon they crossed the creek, the hound let out a howl. The dog went off to the west along the bank, lifting her nose from the scent every few yards.

They followed her several hundred yards along the creek, and there she stopped, having lost the track. Then she splashed through the shallow water and picked up the trail on the other side. Again they followed her to the west, and then the trail led to the north to the forested hillside. A game trail stretched up through the forest and the hound ran along it, hot on the scent.

Thomas led the way until they caught up with the dog. "That little one must have some hillbilly in him. Least he's stickin' to the trails now," the old man said. Ahead of them, the dog whined and would go no further. Off to the left, several yards ahead, they heard the rapid oscillating of a rattler's tail. Jenkins grabbed the rope collar of his hound. "Never seen a dog yet could whip a rattler."

In a few minutes the snake had slithered away from them and Jenkins released the dog. On the top of the ridge they found the boy. He was sitting on a flat rock, gazing off to the north. He started crying when he saw the men. "Going home," he sobbed as Thomas picked him up.

"Going home," Thomas answered. He carried the youngster back down the trail.

Thomas thanked Jenkins, and he and Robert crossed the creek. "You want to find everybody and tell them we've found him?"

"Yeah. I'll find the Dawsons first."

Thomas carried David on his shoulders as he negotiated the trail on the mountain, and in a half hour he was at the mine camp. Mrs. Dawson rushed from the porch when she saw them. She took her son from Thomas and hugged him tightly and the boy began crying again.

"I don't believe he's hurt except for a few scratches. He went through some rough country."

"Thank you," she repeated over and over

Thomas was ready to leave when the Dawson children and their father came running down the trail from above their house. They all crowded around David.

Thomas stood to the side. "I'll be getting back."

"Please come in. Would you like a drink?" Dawson asked.

He started to say no, then looked back to Dawson. Who was Dawson the mine man? "Might be what we need."

Thomas sat on a cushioned chair on the screened porch. Dawson went inside, and Thomas surveyed the room. A woven rug covered the floor. Several chairs faced toward the valley and the Kentucky mountains beyond the Tug River.

Dawson sat down on the chair beside Thomas, set the drinks down, and from his shirt pocket he pulled a crisp twenty-dollar bill. "For your trouble," he said as he held it toward Thomas.

"I didn't have any trouble."

"For finding David. It's times like this that make a man realize how important his family is to him."

"Is twenty dollars all the boy is worth?"

Dawson looked at him in surprise. "Well no, of course not."

"I don't need any money. Besides, it was old man Jenkins and one of his hounds that found the boy. David was a couple of miles from where the kids left him. The hounds tracked him."

"You mean that old man helped find David? He threatened to shoot me if I ever came on his land again. Did he know David was my son?"

"Yes."

Dawson sat bewildered, the twenty-dollar bill in his hand. "I never thought that old man would do anything for me."

"You never needed him to do anything for you. There's still things men will do and not need money for doing it. People around here work together. They always had to work with each other and help each other. That's how we live. Or used to."

"Used to?"

"Still do mostly. But it won't be long before most of the folks see everything boiled down to dollars and cents like you do. There must have been a dozen of the folks looking for David today. They know how important a child is. They'd do the same for anybody, and they'd be insulted if you offered money for helping. Soon as everybody's working for so many dollars and cents a day, and every man is working only for himself, no time to help other folks, then you might have to pay folks to look for a lost boy."

Dawson sat listening, his heavy brows drawn together. "You sound like a philosopher."

Thomas laughed. "I want the best there is for me and my family. You are not here for the reason I am. You got yourself a job and came here for more dollars and cents than you were making before probably."

"Right," Dawson said defensively, wondering how this rough-looking man before him could know about his life.

"Well, now this land is turning into real estate. It's not the same anymore."

"What do you mean, turning into real estate?"

"The land is where a man grows food to feed his family. What he can live from. The land contains all of life past and all the future. A man lives with the land in partnership. But real estate. That's dollars and cents. Real estate is only good for buying and selling."

"That's why you wouldn't sell your land?" Dawson asked. "That sounds fine. But what are we going to do when there are too many people for the land? When your children are grown there won't be enough land in this valley to support them. They'll have to have some way to make money so that they can participate in the advanced economy that only industry can provide."

"I've got no answer for that. What you said may be true. It's what is lost in the process that is bad. People working together and helping each other and living together as neighbors for a purpose will be lost. Neighbors used to be for helping each other. But now they're neighbors only because they somehow ended up living next to each other. You're my neighbor, but the only time I've talked to you until now has been business, dollars and cents. A few years ago if you had come here, me and several other men would have helped you build your home and plant your first crops. But with everything stripped down to dollars and cents, you didn't need any help. I suppose in a way that's good, but it doesn't really make you as self-reliant as it seems. You depend on the coal, not yourself. And you're not a real neighbor that way, 'cause if you don't need any help, then you don't need to help anybody. The way it is now, you could live here for years and never get to know anybody. You'd never need to know anybody, because you wouldn't need anyone. You've never come to me as a neighbor, only as a mine operator. I never knew if you were a man or a mine operator."

They sat in silence, both men feeling strange that they had somehow probed so deeply into each other's thoughts and feelings. "I see your point," Dawson said, breaking the stillness. "But what shall we do in the meantime? I grew up with nothing. I don't intend for my children to do the same."

Thomas laughed, but stopped as he saw the tightness in Dawson's face. "I wasn't laughing at you. But being a mine operator instead of a miner or a hillbilly doesn't make you more important as a man. In God's eyes all these things mean nothing. A man is a man. We're all made of the same stuff, and we'll all end up part of the earth someday."

Dawson's defensiveness turned to curiosity as they talked on. He asked Thomas about his background, wondering especially about his education. Thomas laughed. "It don't take schooling. Ever since my grandmother taught me to read when I was a boy, I've read everything I could get my hands on. Newspapers. Books. Especially about the war. My dad died in sixty-three. Never knew him. I was only five, but my mother and I kept on at the farm with help from our kin and other folks." Thomas gazed out over the river and to the valley beyond.

"I'm sorry," Dawson said.

Thomas waved off the condolence. "Long time ago."

They talked and drank on into the evening. Through their differences, they made contact man to man. As Thomas left, the cool dusk of the August evening stealing over the mountains, he knew that there was more than a mine operator living on the hillside, and Dawson knew likewise that there was more than a hillside dirt farmer living next to him.

Chapter Three
1900

The mines were established. The miners earned good wages and were pleased with the companies that made that wealth possible. The companies were benevolent; they provided the things of life—the food, the shelter, the clothes, the luxuries. All were available with the scrip that each company issued in place of money.

As another year at the mines passed, many came to regard their past lives as inferior and to regard the mountaineers and farmers left in the valleys and mountains as inferior. Being a miner or a member of his family was better than living on some desolate mountainside, many thought.

In the school the new class arrangement began to assert itself. The children of the mine managers always seemed to look brighter and more studious than the other children because of their new, store-bought clothes. Most of the miners' children also fared well, since they were occasionally able to wear the colorful clothes that the company stores kept in stock. But the Greene children and the other mountain children usually wore the same clothes day after day. Never mind that love happened each night, as a mother or an older sister washed the faded overalls or print dresses and hung them to dry on the ridge, or above the fireplace or stove in the winter.

Of the Greene children, Mary was the most distressed by these social developments. She begged Gertrude for new clothes so she could more easily become a member of the most esteemed groups. Gertrude and Mary made new dresses as the family could afford the material, but it was never the same in Mary's eyes. She wanted store-bought clothes. She wanted new, shiny shoes in place of the rough leather ones she worked on each evening to make presentable for the next day.

And slowly but forcibly this socialization took place throughout the mountains and valleys wherever the mines had come. The physical presence of the new order had merely set the process in motion. After that the people made it function, becoming one thing or another—a miner, foreman, weighman, or wives and children of the same—and they competed with each other now more often than they worked together. They saw what a promotion to foreman would make possible for their families. They knew that only money could give them what they needed to survive in this sudden new world of industry.

The men were paid by piecework, so much per ton of coal that each dug. Some made more money than others, either by being better at the tiresome task or by being assigned to the best corridors and coal veins in the mine. But lately all the men's tonnage had begun to be lower than it had been before.

The company employed one man at the tipple as the weighman, and it was the weighman who determined how much coal each man was to be credited for. The loss of tonnage continued for several weeks, and the men saw their weekly pay go down as the reported tonnage decreased. Yet the miners knew they were producing as much or more coal as before.

The talk of the problem grew among the men, and they selected a spokesman, actually a volunteer, since they did not organize to the point of voting for this representative. And their spokesman, a young man named Louis Jenson, who had always been one of the top coal producers, went to Dawson to explain their problem. Dawson heard him out and promised that he would look into the situation.

Dawson never reported back to Jenson, and the weight discrepancies continued. As the weeks went by and September was upon them, many of the men ended up owing the company store money at the end of the pay period. Instead of the usual scrip pay, they found payment due slips in their envelopes. They could no longer purchase their food and pay the monthly rent for their homes with the lowered wages they were suddenly making. And as quickly as it thrust itself upon the people, the social hierarchy that the short time in the mining camp had made possible began to subside. The energy left it. The people were once again striving to survive, and though there was little they could do to help each other in this circumstance, there was once again the cause of survival to unite them, a cause not unlike that which had dominated their former style of life in the hills and valleys. When they had their land they could always come up with some way to forestall the crisis of survival—borrow from their neighbors if they had a poor crop, slaughter one of the hogs early if they ran out of meat, hunt for their food, fish for it, trade for it. Here in the camp they were no longer dependent on themselves; they were dependent on the digging of the coal from the interior of the mountain. They could not borrow from someone who also had nothing. They could not butcher one of their animals if there were none to butcher. They could not nurse a poor crop back to health if there were no crops. There was nothing they could do in their present circumstances. As they slid further into debt each week as their purchases at the store surpassed their wages, their frustrations grew. The men worked harder and increased production, but still they could not make ends meet. They worked longer hours but could not gain any ground. They knew they were being cheated but did not know what to do about it.

Their frustration and bewilderment over their inability to make a living from the mine smoldered into resentment and defensiveness. Their conversations led them nowhere but to a distrust of Dawson and whomever else was involved in cheating them. There came a day in October 1900 when the men did not enter the mine. The first few balked and the others joined them. One man stood on the pile of timbers before the mine entrance.

"I've had enough!" he cried to the group of men milling around. "I'm damn tired of bein' cheated!"

Another miner joined him on the makeshift platform. "They're cheatin' us every day!"

And another joined them. "We wasn't raised to let nobody cheat us. This ain't right."

And the others joined in, shouting agreement to the declarations. One of the foremen ran to get Dawson, who soon arrived at the mine entrance. The men were angry and shouting to be heard. Jenson once again took it upon himself to be their spokesman.

"Now what's the problem?" Dawson asked.

"We're tired of being cheated out of our pay."

"I don't understand," Dawson said. "Who's cheating you out of your pay?"

"You, I guess. Or the weighman or whoever it is you told to cut the weights back."

"You don't really believe that, do you? After you talked to me about the situation, I checked the scales. They calibrated perfectly."

"It ain't the scales."

Grumbles of assent came from the men behind Jenson and Dawson. "What is it then?" Dawson asked.

"If we knew, we'd do somethin' about it. We ain't getting' paid for what we load. We know what a ton of coal looks like."

Dawson, thoroughly confused, looked around at the angry, expectant faces. "You've got to realize that the new vein of coal we've hit carries less weight per volume than the others we've mined here. It can't weigh the same."

"If that's the case then we need more money per ton."

"That's impossible," Dawson said. "If we have to pay too much in wages we'll have to close down. If that happens you'll all be out of work."

The men were silent. They didn't want the mine to close. They had never considered such an occurrence. What could they do? Where could they go if that happened?

"How about if you put one of us with the weighman, just so's we can make sure we're getting paid for what comes out?" Jenson said. "We don't want the mine to close down. We'll pay the man ourselves." He turned to the group of men behind him. "Anybody object to that? Us payin' one of our men to help with the weighin'?"

"Sounds all right to me," one of the men said and the others followed suit.

Dawson frowned. "No. That's not possible."

"It ain't going to cost you nothin'," Jenson said.

"No. I can't authorize that." He couldn't go to Harris with a proposition like the men were making. Dawson spoke louder now, "You men are not running the mine. I am. Whatever I say is the way it's going to be. If you don't like it here then get out. There's coal to be dug. Any of you who want to work, get going. Any man who stays out is fired." With that, Dawson turned and walked away.

The men were quiet and Jenson addressed them. "We got to stick together. If we all stay out, they can't do nothin'."

The miners talked among themselves, considering their choice of going to work or staying out and risking their jobs. "I ain't got nowhere else to go," one man said and walked toward the entrance.

"What we supposed to live on if we don't dig no coal? I got to work."

"Got to feed the family," another said.

One at a time, then by twos and threes, the men entered the mine. The last to enter the black hole was Jenson.

Two days later, on the same day the sheriff served him with an eviction notice, Louis Jenson was fired. He had five days in which to find another place for his family to live. "Union man," the rumor had effectively been circulated, even though the United Mine Workers organizers had not made any headway in the southern West Virginia coalfields. "Jenson's a union man." Associating with him would mean complicity, would mean risking one's job. Jenson was alone.

He left the camp for a couple of days that week seeking work in one of the other mines downriver. Most of the mines usually needed men and he was optimistic as he set out to look for work. He scoured the area looking for a job, but the answer was the same at all the mines he visited. "No jobs," the operators all told him. "No jobs for agitators," one operator came right out and told him. He was blacklisted.

The operators and owners knew what unionization would do to their bottom line. Any talk of organizing the men was equated with sabotage and violence. Most of the miners were also, though for different reasons from the operators, against any talk of unions. They were independent people. A formal organization like a union was something they had never known or needed. They had always fought their own battles in these mountains and thought they would continue to do so.

A man stood up for himself. They had learned that well in the mountains. But they did not know, could not know or understand the workings of the newly arrived industrial system. Supply and demand? A union to bargain for them? You dug a ton of coal or plowed a hillside and planted it. You and the mattock or the horse and plow. Nothing else.

Thomas had heard from the stories that his children brought from school that a man was being evicted. The teachers had discussed the events in the schoolroom. "Mr. Kent said when a man works for a mine he's got to cooperate," Robert told him. "He said we all got to learn to get along with people that's our bosses."

"He was making trouble, the teacher said," James told Thomas of Jenson.

Thomas had not heard the full story and had not seen Dawson for several weeks. But he didn't concern himself. Not until Louis Jenson came to Thomas to try to trade some goods for a horse did Thomas hear the story firsthand. Jenson had built a sled, which he would use to haul his furniture away. "Got a stove and a revolver I can trade," he told Thomas. "The stove's paid for. I can trade it. Made the last payment a couple of months ago."

"Come on in and sit awhile," Thomas invited him. Thomas learned the story of what had happened as they sat drinking spring water. Jenson had decided to return to the hollow upriver from which he had come. But he would not stay there long. He still wanted to work in a mine somewhere. He liked the work and $1.50 a day would support him and his family.

"My kids are going to live where they can get some schoolin'. I reckon I'll be going downriver to look for work. Probably end up in the city. But I can't do nothin' special. I hate to go where I don't know nothin' about what to do."

Thomas promised that he would help get Jenson's belongings loaded and arranged a trade for the horse. And shortly Jenson was on his way, a fresh-baked loaf of bread and a ham tucked under his arm. Thomas didn't have any pressing work for himself that day. The corn, a good crop this year, wouldn't be ready for harvest for another week. He finished his water and went outside to where Robert was cleaning out the chicken coop. He could help with the moving.

Shortly, Thomas and Robert were walking along the railroad, Robert leading the ten-year-old horse, now a gelding, the first colt Thomas and his father-in-law Gabriel Ransom had acquired through their horse breeding operation, which brought in most of their cash money. His brother-in-law Matthew had been using the horse for plowing and cultivating this year and had the week before told Thomas to sell it first chance he got. They passed the growing slag heap, which had spread along the base of the hill and toward the railroad tracks so far that there was barely room to pass. They walked the grade that led to the dusty strip that split the mine camp in half.

Thomas watched a chair hit and shatter on the pile of furniture in the street. Then he saw Louis Jenson sitting at one end of the porch, blood smeared over his face. Two small children, and a woman holding a baby, stood beside Jenson. Thomas saw, as he ran to the porch, that Jenson was handcuffed to the railing.

"What happened?" Thomas asked him.

"The sheriff," he said through puffy lips. "I told 'em I was leaving but they wouldn't hear me out. They're bustin' up everthing I've got."

Two burly men with holstered revolvers on their hips were carrying a table through the doorway. Then they stood on the porch, rocking the table back and forth. It hit on its side, splintering two of the legs off.

Several women and children from other camp families watched the eviction from a safe distance. Down the street, the men were coming out of the mine at the end of their shift.

Thomas stepped onto the porch.

"Just keep out of the way," the sheriff told Thomas as he threw several pans onto the heap in the street and turned back into the house.

"We came to help this man move," Thomas said. "We'll finish the job."

"Supposed to been out by yesterday evenin'. You ain't siding with that damn agitator, are you?" the deputy answered.

"We'll help him move. You don't need to bust up any more of his things."

"Just upholdin' the law. Now you get on out of the way or you'll be under arrest just like that one over there."

"What's he arrested for?"

"Interfering with an officer of the law. He grabbed hold of one of my deputies."

The miners were coming up the street now. Several of them gathered around the porch and were watching as the sheriff grabbed Thomas from behind. A deputy hit Thomas in the stomach and doubled him over, then struck him in the face. "Now you're under arrest too," the sheriff said. "Give me them other handcuffs," he ordered his deputy.

Thomas's hands were cuffed behind his back and a deputy pushed him to the porch floor.

Thomas struggled to sit up and turned to the men standing around the porch. "You're next!" he shouted.

The sheriff pulled a long club out of his belt and hit the back of Thomas's head.

Robert had stood back, too frightened and confused to do anything. Now he rushed blindly through the group of men, the tears rolling down his face. Up the stairs he went and then he was clawing at the sheriff's holster. "I'll kill you!" he shouted. The sheriff knocked the boy away. Another deputy picked Robert up and dropped him over the porch railing.

One of the men shouted, "Jenson ain't no union man! I lived up the same holler with him all my life!"

"This ain't right!" another shouted.

The miners surged onto the porch as a group. The sheriff and one of the deputies went down, but the other deputy moved to the side of the porch and drew his gun. His hand shook as he pointed the gun at the writhing mass of men. "I'll shoot ya! Let them men go!" he shouted.

By now the sheriff had been relieved of his gun. "He's got my gun," came his muffled cry.

A shot was fired, the deputy was clubbed from behind, and his gun dropped onto the porch. The miners dragged the deputies off the porch and threw them into the street. A couple of the others carried the wounded miner from the porch. A woman's cry cut the air and she knelt beside her husband, now lying next to the debris pile. The men emptied from the porch.

Robert searched the sheriff's pockets for the keys to the handcuffs. Someone held Thomas up and Robert unlocked the cuffs. A woman brought a pan of water and cleaned up the gash on Thomas's head.

Dawson now stood in the street, looking at the blood spattered down the porch steps. The sheriff and his deputies lay unconscious.

A rifle was thrust into Dawson's back. "What the hell's going on?" Dawson said in amazement and turned to face the man.

"How'd you like that to be your furniture all busted up?" a man shouted into his face.

Most of the men were armed now. Some carried rifles or pistols; others carried shotguns or ancient long-barreled guns. Down the street they moved as a group, Dawson pushed roughly along before them. The company weighman was found. One of the men held a rifle to his head. "Now you start talkin'."

The man's eyes were wide with fear. He looked at Dawson, then at the men. He started crying, holding his face with the open palms of his hands. "Go ahead and shoot," he sobbed. "I done it. Mr. Harris, he said he'd give me part of whatever I could cut off the weights. He give me fifty dollars to start." The weighman looked up at the grimy faces all round him. Silence replaced the anger and Dawson shook his head, not believing.

The man holding the rifle to the weighman's face lowered it.

"You ain't worth killin'. You ain't worth shit. You get out of here. You get out."

The men were coming back up the street in twos and threes, beginning to realize the consequences of what they had done. But there was no fear in their hearts. The blood of mountaineers past flowed through these coal-tattooed men, blood of the bold, free mountain men or of the one-generation-free slaves or of the quiet foreigners recruited from the cities. But it flowed with a strength and purpose; these were free men.

Chapter Four

The men did not return to the mine. They were waiting to see how the new justice would work. Dawson had promised that he would take care of the problems, ascertain how much pay had been lost, and make it up to them. The miner who had been shot was assured by Dawson that he could live in the company house until he was able to return to work.

But as he made these promises to the men, Dawson realized that he had a problem; he would have to clear his decisions with Harris, and he also had to confront Harris with the accusations that the weighman had made. Was Harris really a crook? Dawson asked himself over and over. The other mine managers told Dawson to just fire the troublemakers and get on with business, but Dawson couldn't make himself take that advice.

Dawson considered quitting his job, but decided against it. He would get to the bottom of the problem. If Harris didn't like his methods or decisions, then let Harris fire him. He sent a wire to Harris in Pittsburgh the same day of the disturbance. "Please come at once. Major decisions concerning coal weights and wages to be made," it read after he had written and discarded several versions. He could not confront Harris with the accusation by wire. Let Harris come here, he thought, and face to face he would deal with the owner.

The sheriff came back a week later with several unnamed warrants, which the county judge had readily issued. He sought out Dawson to name the men to be arrested.

"I don't believe the men are at fault," Dawson told the sheriff.

"The hell. You let this bunch of rabble get away with it this time ... you saw what they did to us," he said, fingering the still bruised side of his face. "Nobody's goin' to assault the law and get away with it. Not in this county. That feller that started all this. I want him." He folded all the warrants but one and slapped it onto the desk. "Write his name in there. The rest of them can go to hell if that's the way you want it."

Dawson sat at his desk and pictured Thomas Greene. He owed him. Besides, the man who had really started the trouble was Harris. "I don't know who started it," Dawson said. "I wasn't there."

The sheriff stood for before the desk. "You don't know what the hell you're doing. Protecting that bunch of Reds out there who tried to take over this camp. Next time ... don't send for me next time. You're on your own now. You're chicken-shit."

The miners sat on their porches watching the sheriff and his men ride out. Inside most of their doors were the guns they had gotten and loaded when they had seen the men ride into town. They would fight if they had to. No formal agreement had been reached among them. They acted independently, as one mind with the same purpose—to defend their homes and their freedom.

"Chicken-shit, he called me," Dawson said to Thomas, laughing out of his nervousness. Dawson had received the wire back from Harris saying that he would not come, that Dawson would have to make his own decisions. He had found himself walking along the tracks, seeking out Thomas Greene. He wanted to go over the events with Thomas, and also alert him that the sheriff was looking for him.

"He doesn't know where to look," Thomas told him. "And from the sound of it, he won't be around here again. But what about Louis Jenson?"

"He's still got a job if he wants it," Dawson said. "As weighman. I feel rotten about this whole thing. Harris tried to cheat the men, and I got caught in the middle. Harris won't even come out here to accept any of the responsibility for this. He put it on my shoulders. I'm going to make it up to the men."

The next day was a Sunday, and the word was spread that Dawson wanted to talk to all the men in the camp. They gathered near his office and listened to him, warily assessing his promises. He gave each man enough credit at the company store to account for the lost wages from the last couple of months. He told them Jenson would be the new weighman. And then a foreman went into the small office and carried a barrel of beer outside. For the first time since he had been at the camp, Dawson got to know some of the men who worked for him. They were different from him. That was obvious to all. But they were all men. That was all. Nothing more than men looking to make the best life possible for themselves and their families. Equal men. They would all die someday; there would be no difference then. The seed that Thomas Greene had planted in Dawson grew. He was a reasonable and honest man, unusual for a mine manager in these brutal coalfields. He wanted to be fair, and most of the men accepted his overtures of friendship that afternoon.

By five o'clock the horseshoes were leaning against a post, the board targets lay in splinters against the hillside, and the men gathered in the shade of the oaks around the office. The beer was gone, and the moonshine started around the circle of miners sitting on stacks of timbers. Before long they were indeed equals. Dawson's and Jenson's children were the first to show up in the boisterous group.

"Momma said supper's ready," Jenson's girl Martha told her dad and tugged on his belt.

Dawson's boy David stood before his blurry-eyed father and Dawson got the message too. The women had not known there would be drinking, especially after church on a Sunday, and as they saw what was happening kept a close eye on the group. Other children came and sat with their dads and soon the group had broken up, leaving three hardcore drinkers sitting in a circle smoking and passing the jug.

Dawson had met the challenge and had solved the differences with his men. He realized now that he owed allegiance to more than just Harris and the other, smaller stockholders. He owed as much to the men working in the mine, and frequently thereafter he could be found in one corridor or another of the mine, wearing work clothes now, talking to his men, assessing firsthand the problems and difficulties they encountered. And under Dawson's leadership, the mining town thrived.

Thomas read often in the Williamson Daily News of the labor troubles plaguing the Tug Valley mine camps and the rest of southern West Virginia. Disputes over the weighing procedures were common, along with incidents over the eviction of men who were maimed in the many cave-ins and coal dust explosions. The unions that were already being established in the northern coalfields were attempting to gain a foothold in the southern West Virginia coalfields. Any man who talked about the unions, or dared to join one, was fired and blacklisted.

At Mine #3, Dawson had insisted from the first that the mine be made as safe as possible. He now handled complaints from the men not as anarchy but as suggestions to be seriously considered.

Thomas and Dawson became even better friends. Often Dawson would use Thomas as a sounding board for his ideas about managing the mine. There grew an understanding between the two, and they were able to learn from each other.

Dawson heard from Harris infrequently. Dawson's production reports were impressive, as was his safety record. There were no reports of down time from labor problems at Mine #3. The only thing approaching a problem for Dawson had come during the audit when Harris demanded an explanation of the loss of profit from the company store during the fall of 1900. Dawson wrote back, after much thought, that he had found that the scales were out of calibration and that he had made the appropriate adjustments in the men's pay. Harris accepted the explanation. And so it went at Mine #3. The promised prosperity descended upon the valley, and a couple of the miners bought horses from Gabriel and Thomas, and these were stabled for a charge at Gabriel's farm. Some of the men saved their money, others sent money back home to their less fortunate relations, while others spent every nickel they earned and accumulated machines and other goods. Of course, none of this use of their earnings would have been possible unless Dawson had started the practice of redeeming the scrip pay at full cash value.

One man even bought a huge, steel wringer-washer for his wife. But it quit working after six months, and parts were not available. So it sat on their front porch like a bowlegged beast of unknown origin, collecting a coat of reddish-black rust from the weather and coal dust. Others spent their extra money for liquor. On Saturday nights in the camp the liquor flowed. As the camaraderie had developed among the men, as their jobs grew increasingly dangerous as they picked and hammered and augured and blasted their way deeper into the mountain, as the cave-ins and accidents increased and men were without some of their fingers, or unable to see from one eye, or deaf in one ear or both, as they collected the scars of their trade and wore the fine gray coal tattoo of the miner in all the pores of their bodies, there was increasingly good reason for many of them to drink, to blot out the mine for at least one night of the week, and to obliterate the ever-present danger and fatigue.

In February of 1902, one of the workers lost his arm in a collision of two of the cars that were used to transport the coal out of the mine. There was no provision made by the company for a man who was hurt so badly he could not work anymore. The standard procedure was for the crippled miner to be evicted from his home at the camp. But Mine #3 had really quit following standard procedure ever since Dawson had made amends to the wronged miners in the fall of 1900. The injured man, George Poland, could not again work in the mines or in any of the other jobs that were available in the mountains. The man's oldest son was only ten and could sort slag, but that wouldn't pay the rent.

The injured miner had nowhere to go. He could not leave his home to look for land. He didn't have enough money to buy land. He could not really do anything until his shoulder had healed itself from the amputation. Dawson discussed the problem with Thomas, and again Thomas helped out by offering to let Poland build a house on his land. But they still had to find a place for him to live until the house could be built. Dawson finally told him he could stay in the company house until the new home could be built on the west edge of Thomas's land. And the mine company, Dawson decided, would supply all the building materials if Thomas could organize the manpower.

As soon as the weather broke in early March, Thomas and Robert, John Hatfield, and numerous of Thomas's cousins and uncles, along with the miners and the mine management, each evening took turns working together to build the new home for Poland, who also helped with the work as he could. There were so many people helping that they often got in each other's way. But in a couple of weeks, when the house was finished, nearly every man and woman in the valley could say that they had taken part in the building, and after the grateful miner and his family moved into the house, a celebration was planned.

Thomas was happy with the outcome, and this experience, along with his conversations with Dawson, softened his attitude to the coming of the mines. It all depended, he knew, as did any venture undertaken by man, on who was in charge. But Thomas also knew, and this is what made him retain his cynical view of the changes being wrought, that not all men would have handled the situation as intelligently and reasonably as had Dawson. Indeed, stories were told by travelers and in the newspapers of men who were evicted from their homes after injures such as this: blind men, armless or legless men, angry, helpless men and their families shoved from their homes onto the street and hurried on their way by the sheriff or company guards.

As the spring weather once again fully embraced the mountains and valleys and as the plans for the celebration were made and men and women were assigned to bring the various items needed, the hogs to butcher and roast, the cornbread, the vegetables, and the pies and cakes, the people of the valley worked together and were united. Mrs. Dawson organized the miners' wives and the other managers' wives, and they talked Dawson out of enough lumber to build the long tables on which the food would be placed, and a spirit of oneness and togetherness flooded the people's hearts. Never had this valley seen such a celebration, though it had known the sharing. Thomas was elated as he witnessed the spirit in the people, and as the anticipation of the feast grew.

Saturday was the day of the celebration. Tuesday, Dawson received a wire from Harris saying that he would soon be in Mingo County to implement some changes in the operation of the mines. Dawson was disheartened at this information, but with the expectation and planning of the celebration he would not allow this coincidental visit to dampen his spirits. Whatever happened between him and Harris was bound to happen sooner or later, he knew. On Thursday, Dawson received a wire advising that Harris would be coming on the train on Friday evening.

Dawson had made expenditures for which he had not received clearance. The lumber for the new home and the tables was unauthorized, as was the donation by the company store of the many staples it was providing for Saturday's celebration. But Dawson quickly dismissed his feelings of concern. Harris had made it clear at one time that he should make whatever expenditures he thought necessary. And Harris couldn't argue with the production record of the mine, though Dawson knew he might have to prove that the lumber for Poland's house was in some way aiding that production. Dawson had already proved it for himself. After they started work on the house, production had risen five per cent above its former level.

The planning went on. Harris arrived Friday afternoon on the coal train. He was a big man, well over six feet tall, muscular and healthy. Dawson helped him get settled into the guesthouse that had been readied by several of the camp women that week.

Later, Harris came over to the Dawson house for dinner. As Mrs. Dawson worked in the kitchen finishing the meal preparation, the men sat in the living room drinking some of the whiskey that Thomas had gotten upon Dawson's request. Harris took a sip of the caramel-colored stuff and licked the rich drink from his lips. Then he lifted the tumbler to his nose and smelled it. "That's about the best whiskey I ever tasted," he said and looked at Dawson. "Is that from our store? I didn't know we stocked anything this good."

Dawson laughed. "That's some of our homegrown whiskey."

"Maybe I should be in the whiskey business instead of mining. I'll bet you could trade these hillbillies out of a barrel of this stuff pretty easy." He sipped it again and shook his head.

Before Dawson could answer, but his wife called them to dinner. As he followed Harris into the dining room, watching the man's graceful, lumbering strides, he wondered how Harris would react to the news of the celebration tomorrow. Dawson had a sinking feeling. He knew Harris could not understand what was going on. How could a man who tried to cheat the men out of their wages understand anything but dollars and cents? Thinking in dollars and cents. Helping people. Let it come, then, he thought. Let Harris think what he might.

There was a growing strength in Dawson. Since he had come to these mountains, a subtle but gradual change had occurred within him. He felt more at ease, happier than he had ever been in his life. Perhaps it was the good wages he was earning by managing the mine. Or his relationship with the employees there. He always felt good when they greeted him, as he saw that they were prospering at their jobs. They were prospering together. And the men knew that they were not entirely on their own. Many of them had told him how they felt about the help he had given Poland. Now they knew that if they were disabled, Dawson would come through for them and their families. Or perhaps it was the mountains, with their abundance of life and the peace they could bestow upon a man. Or his family. His wife's contentedness. His children who were healthy and happy in their lives here. Or all these things together.

Chapter Five

Harris had explained, as he and Dawson sat in the living room, that he was pleased with the way things had gone at Mine #3; it had the least problems of any of the mines and had out-produced the others. But Harris also mentioned that he had a few ideas about cutting costs that he was planning to implement in all his mines. The demand for coal was down at the present time. Prices had dropped, and to maintain the level of profit of the first few years, a few corners would have to be cut. But Harris did not name any specific areas of reduction in spending. "That can wait until tomorrow," he said.

Harris was awakened in the morning by the sounds of hammering from somewhere down the hillside. He could not see anyone working as he stood on the porch in the crisp, spring air. He had declined Mrs. Dawson's offer to have breakfast with them. After stoking the fire in the stove, he had his coffee and the pastry Mrs. Dawson had made for him.

Dawson was waiting for him, as they planned to tour the mine and loading facilities and to go over the changes Harris wanted to implement. As soon as they started down the hill, Harris asked,

"What the hell's all the commotion over there?" He could see the men working and the smoke from the pits in which the pork was roasting.

"There's a celebration today. A sort of housewarming, I guess you'd call it."

"Looks like a good day for it," Harris said. "Is the weather always this good around here? Hell, we've still got snow in Pittsburgh." The air felt clean and fresh. A light rain had fallen during the night, the few patches of cottony, leftover clouds sparking silvery-white in the warming sun.

"We get a lot of rain this time of year. It always seems pleasant enough, though."

"What sort of celebration is it, did you say? A housewarming?"

"It's a sort of get-together for everyone in the valley. They all helped build a house for one of the men who was injured in the mine."

Harris stood on one of the timber steps, looking toward the newly constructed house and the preparations in the distance. "You mean he's got his own house and everything and doesn't even work anymore? That doesn't make much sense. What's he got, rich relatives or something?" Harris laughed.

"That's just the way people are around here. They look out for each other. It was hard for me to understand at first too. They stick together. It's different from the cities. You know, everything there is boiled down to dollars and cents."

"What?" Harris asked.

"Nothing."

Harris glanced at Dawson as they continued down the steps. "I'd like you to take over management of all three mines. Could you handle it?"

Surprised, Dawson stared at Harris, as if making sure he was serious.

"You've done a good job here. The other managers would stay on as foremen and day to day managers. You would probably only need one day a week of travel to do what I have in mind. There will be a raise for you."

"I can do it."

"Good," Harris answered, then seemed to forget the praise he had just given Dawson.

"Did you paint all the houses already?" Harris asked, looking at the bright homes in the distance.

"Yes. Well, I gave the men the paint. They did the work themselves."

Harris cleared his throat and spat. "That's one thing we can save money on. What did it cost for the paint?"

"If I remember right it was about $170.00."

Harris pursed his lips. "That's a lot of money to waste. Whose idea was that?"

"Mainly the men's, I guess. And mine. Several of them were asking me about it, and the houses were looking gray, so I told them I'd give them the paint." Below them the mine camp had taken on the appearance of a friendly village. Most men, actually their wives and children, had chosen white, but there was also a blue house and two red ones.

"OK, no more paint. Let them buy their own from now on. And why the hell aren't you operating today?" Harris blurted, suddenly realizing that no one was working his mine.

"First Saturday we haven't worked in a year. We're all due for a day off."

Harris shook his head in amazement. There was nothing to be said, though. Dawson was his best manager.

They continued down the hill, and Dawson stopped at his office to get a couple of lamps for the mine inspection.

Dawson led him into the black entrance and down the corridor that led off to the right. This was the best area of the mine. The rooms off to the sides of the main shaft were well timbered to prevent cave-ins. "Oh no," Harris said, shaking his head after they had toured a couple of the rooms. "You are using too many timbers. Half that many will do."

Dawson frowned and looked at Harris. "That's the number I found will give the most safety. You can't get production from an injured man."

"You don't *need* production from an injured man."

They went on in silence, Harris occasionally remarking about the excessive numbers of timbers.

"I've seen enough," Harris said after a few more minutes. "Have to stay bent over too much in here. Gets my back after a while."

They left the mine and went back to Dawson's office. Harris sat down at the desk. "OK. We've got to cut about ten percent of the costs of running the mine. Raise all the prices in the store by ten percent. Don't spend anything on repairs on the houses. No more damn paint … and you can cut the number of timbers you use. And …."

"I won't cut back on the timbers," Dawson said. "The slate is too brittle. It breaks up easy. If I cut back on timbers, then we're going to get a lot of men needlessly hurt."

Harris sat staring at Dawson. "Look. Our profits were cut nearly in half last month. If prices keep dropping, we'll be in trouble. I'm not suggesting that you stop using so many timbers. I'm telling you. That's an order. You do it. Now to get ten percent back we're going to have to cut wages somehow. Cutting back on timbers and maintenance and raising prices at the store might save one or two percent. That's a start." Harris leaned back in the chair and locked his hands behind his head. "Have you got any ideas on how we can cut wages?"

Dawson had considered the problem before and thought he had come up with a solution. "If I explain the problem to the men, I think we can work it out. I'll make up a schedule that will make their wages fluctuate up and down as coal prices go up and down. That way they'll get paid according to the same schedule of profit that the market forces on us. It would mean a lot of extra work in computing their pay, but I can handle it."

"Oh, bullshit," Harris said slowly. "What're you talking about?"

Dawson stared calmly at Harris. "I'm talking about an idea. A damn good one, the way I see it. Make the men part of the business."

"Maybe you don't see quite as clearly as you think you do. What are we going to do when we get a good market again? We'd be paying them all the profits when the prices go up."

"We can put bottom and top limits on their wages. That way unless something drastic happens, the men know what to expect. That's all they want. To know what to expect out of us."

"The men, the men! Who the hell are you working for? Me or them?"

"Both of you, I guess. You pay me my wages. They dig the coal. I need you both."

"You talk like we've got to come to some kind of agreement with them. The miners don't have it that good up north with their damn unions."

Dawson looked at the splintery wood floor. "I was just trying to come up with a fair solution. What's your idea?"

"Once you give these guys something, they'll want more. When they start wanting more, they'll end up with a bunch of damn union agitators running around here. They're already covering the state. United Mine Workers. Knights of Labor.

Passing out their damn books. They'll be around here pretty quick. What do you think will happen if we get a union in here?"

"They've already been here. Many times," Dawson said. "The men ran them off."

"Ran them off?"

"Yes. I've treated them fairly so far. They know they can trust me. They don't need a union if they can get a fair shake."

Harris shook his head slowly back and forth. "Do you really believe that?" Before Dawson could answer, Harris continued. "Who's your weighman now? Can you trust him?"

"Yes. I trust him. He's been here since the mine opened. Started out in the mine, but a couple of years ago I gave him the job."

"I mean, will he knock off some of the weight? Will he take a bribe to rig the scales?"

"In other words, you want me to cheat the men out of their wages?"

"If you want to look at it that way. It's the easiest way to cut back wages. Hell, most of the mines started out that way. The men never know the difference after that. That was our biggest mistake, not starting out with the scale rigged. I can't complete with companies that have an automatic five or ten percent edge over me."

"Well, at least you're telling me about it this time," Dawson said, looking Harris in the eye. Dawson knew he was on dangerous ground now. But let it come, he thought. Dawson would not, could not, do what Harris was asking him to do. He remembered the day he met Harris. He had thought at the time he was meeting one of the great men of the business world. There was a smoothness about the man, a calculating sort of intelligence that was helpful in running a successful business. And the man's size contributed. He conveyed strength of mind and body to those around him.

Dawson looked around his office. The engineering books on the rough board shelves. Ledgers, accounting books, the files. The small stove in the corner behind the desk where Harris was sitting. Harris could not know the simple comfort of entering this ramshackle office on a blustery winter day, with the small cast stove glowing red-hot in the corner, sending out in waves its cozy warmth. He could not know how it felt to have the men in the mine respect him because they knew that he was honest and would give them a fair decision in any matter.

Dawson stared at this large-boned, handsome man, looking so at ease and so casual sitting at the desk discussing the various ways to cheat men out of their wages. Greed, that's what it was. What else would drive a man to cheat and force men into a situation that was not beneficial to them? Dawson suddenly despised Harris. He didn't know him, had never really gotten to know him. Dollars and cents had brought him here. Dollar and cents had brought both of them here. Purposeless, mindless devotion to dollars and cents. And the men. The same thing had brought them here. The desire for more money. But the men in the mine only wanted to live. What could Harris possibly do with all the money he had made from these mines? Why did he need more and more?

"What do you mean 'this time'?" Harris snapped, suddenly sitting upright.

"Didn't you ever wonder what happened to our other weighman here?"

"I don't follow the employees. That's your job."

"That's right. And as long as I'm here, I'll see that the weighman gives each man due credit for what he digs."

"Do you want to keep your job here?"

"Yes."

"You let me know by this afternoon how you're going to cut the wages. It'll be done with or without you." Harris stood up.

"If I cut the wages, will they be raised again when the coal price goes up?"

"What the hell's the matter with you?" Harris stormed. "I'm not Rockefeller. Everything I've got is tied up in these mines. If I lose here, I'm done."

Dawson started to answer, to say that the workers also had everything tied up in this mine, including their lives, but Harris had already started for the door.

Dawson caught up with him on the hillside. Harris turned to him. "Look. So far you've done an excellent job. I'd like to keep you here or I wouldn't have offered you full responsibility for all three mines. But I won't hesitate to replace you. You understand that? I'll be leaving about five this afternoon. It's the only train going all the way to Williamson. Let me know before then what you decide."

Dawson didn't answer. He had already decided. He wouldn't let Harris push him into doing something that would not only violate the simplest sense of decency, but would also bring trouble to the mine. Harris could not understand these men working at the mine. Their fierce independence. Their heritage of sticking together in hard times. Leave it until later, Dawson told himself, and turned his thoughts to the coming festivities of the day.

The area around the new home was congested. Several men were finishing the tables, others tending to the barbecue pits, children swarming around it all, excited after the weeks of anticipation. "Do you want to come this afternoon?" Dawson asked Harris as they stood watching the preparations.

Harris turned to him and laughed. "You mean you're going? I thought you said it was for the people in the valley."

"I'm one of the people. Why don't you come? It will give you a chance to get to know the men working for you."

Harris shook his head, laughing without answering as they reached Dawson's house.

Dawson stood looking after him, and then went inside.

Dawson and his wife went down the hill about noon. The children had gone down earlier in the morning. They would not eat for a couple of hours as there were many events planned. Games and foot races for the children. Rifle and pistol shooting for the men and boys. Horseshoes. Most of the women were finishing their preparations.

The shooting was what brought Harris down the hill. He heard the shots and first thought there was trouble. He grew curious as he heard the cheers and shouts from below. When Harris reached the festivities, he saw Dawson holding a revolver with both hands, aiming at a target on the mountain base. Thomas was standing beside him, instructing him in the use of the weapon.

Harris walked along the food-laden tables and past the smoking barbecue pits. Several people nodded greetings to him or spoke. Harris watched as Dawson squeezed the trigger, and the revolver pulled his hands and arms upward. Dawson and the men around him were laughing. "Hold your breath when you squeeze the trigger," one of the called out. Dawson fired the other five rounds and handed the gun to the man standing next to him. "That's enough for me," he laughed, and turned back to Thomas. Then he saw Harris standing behind him.

"Come over and join us," he called, surprised to see Harris. "Want to try your luck?"

"Well, it's been awhile since I've shot one of them. Forty-five?" he asked the miner who had holstered the revolver Dawson had been firing.

"Yep," the man answered. "Want to give her a try?"

Harris took the reloaded gun and aimed at the board target. He took careful aim on the first two shots, squeezing them off gently, then fired the rest in rapid succession.

"Ain't bad for a city feller," the man said, taking the smoking gun back.

"Will you be eating with us?" Dawson asked him. "I can introduce you to the men."

"I don't think."

"Got plenty of food here," Thomas broke in. "The pork is done."

"I'll eat with you," Harris finally said.

They stood to the side, watching the other men shoot. Then the word was spread that all was ready. The people gathered around the tables before the house. Gabriel stood on the porch. He had volunteered to give the prayer. Those finishing the meal preparation stopped their labors, the children were quieted, and all was still as Gabriel began: "Dear Lord, we are gathered today to eat of the food You have provided. We are grateful. We ask Your continued guidance for this man, whose home was built by everyone gathered here, and with Your help. We pray that the spirit of love that helped us build this home remains in our hearts. We ask Your blessing for these two special men who contributed most to this occasion. Thomas Greene for donating his land, and Mr. Dawson for giving us the lumber and other materials to build this house."

Dawson glanced at Harris as Gabriel said "Amen." His brows were drawn together. Then his jaw was clenched and his face reddening. Let it come, Dawson thought. And he smiled broadly at the dumbstruck Harris.

"Shall I introduce you to the men now?" Dawson asked him.

"You're a fool. You're finished."

After Harris left that evening on the coal train, Dawson spread the word that he would no longer be the manager of the mine. He had waited to tell the men, because he was afraid of what might happen to Harris when the men found out what had transpired. Many of them had been drinking all day, and though they were amiable enough in their groups at the celebration, Dawson knew the liquor could give to the day an ending that he did not wish to see.

A dozen men crowded around him in disbelief. "Why?" "What for?" "It ain't right." They worked the best mine in the Tug Valley. They produced the most coal. Dawson helped them produce. He watched over them. He cared and looked out for them and their families.

The mine engineer who lived on the hill next to Dawson had been appointed temporary manager.

But no major changes were planned in the operation until Harris could find the right man for the job.

Chapter Six
1903

Thomas and Gertrude sat by the fire that Thomas had stoked in the fireplace before anyone else had gotten up. As had become his custom over the years, he had risen long before the other members of the family. He had also rekindled the fire in the stove for the family's breakfast. Outside, the darkness of a spring morning was fast giving way to dawn.

But for the recent peace that had settled over the mines, he and Gertrude, and the other residents of the valley, had begun to feel as if they were living on a battlefield. At any moment there was the possibility of violence, murder, the eviction of honest men from their homes. They were not a part of it, but it affected them; just as the coal dust crept under their door sills or through the cracks in the shells of their log dwellings, the tenseness and brutality of the coalfields crept into their lives. All were affected, all forced to choose sides.

The violence of the last several years had taken its toll. Defeated, haggard, landless men had taken the place of the independent mountaineers who had come to the mines for work. It was a tortured land now, marching to the frenzied cadence of the industrial world. Thomas pictured the land he had always loved. The solitude and beauty. The people. The presence of God in all things that met the eye. These had been disturbed, if not ruined, for eternity. If the world were really going to end, as the Bible told, Thomas imagined this monstrosity called industry a good start.

Gertrude came to him and sat with him, the crackling of the warming fire gently breaking the stillness, and her embrace was like a fresh breath to him. He held her until they heard the children stirring about, and she set about preparing the family's breakfast.

William lay on his cot in the loft. He lifted the leather flap that covered the hole between the logs, a thin shaft of cold air pushing into the room, and looked across the field. He had chipped the mortar away so he could observe the world that awaited him each morning. In the distance, past the field, he could see one of the Barker children fetching in the morning's wood. The Barkers were one of the families that Thomas had allowed to live on his land. It was hard for William to understand Jamie Barker's feelings of animosity toward him and the other Greene children. Hadn't Thomas done them a good turn by letting them build their cabin on his land? He knew it was so. Thomas had told him that folks who had always made their own way don't like being beholden to other folks. That had helped William understand why Jamie was so mean to them, but it didn't really settle anything.

William let the flap fall back across the hole. He dressed and made his bed. Richard was already up and gone. William's thoughts turned to the coming school day. He had been chosen to read the morning story to the younger children while the teachers started the older ones with their daily assignments. He would read his story first, the one he had written, before he began reading out of the storybook. Anticipating the morning at school, he descended the ladder from the loft.

The day always started in a busy, exciting whirl. The chores to be done before school. The breakfast with all the family gathered around. William felt especially good this morning.

"Sleepyhead!" Robert called to him. "Hurry up and get the eggs."

"I'm going. I'm going," William mumbled as he pulled his jacket from the peg near the back door. He always resented Robert telling him what to do. It wasn't his place. The brisk air felt good to him as he trotted out to the chicken house. He opened the door to be greeted by the noisy clucking. "All right," he told the hens as they flapped at him from their roosts. "Get on out of here."

At breakfast, they planned a fishing trip for after school to Steep Gut Creek. The suckers were biting, Poland had walked over to tell Thomas the evening before. As William left for school, he knew it would be a good day. Everything felt right today. Violet and Mary and Richard were with him as he led the way down the trail to the railroad tracks.

He heard the train coming before he saw it. He could ride to school today. The coal trains had lately begun their siding pickups earlier in the day as the number of mines increased. He looked over his shoulder, and Mary met his glance.

"I'm telling if you get on that train again today. You know how dangerous Momma said it is. I'll tell," she threatened.

"I only did it once before."

"Once too much. Now you stay off it."

They reached the cinder path that stretched along the railroad. William and the others waved at the engineer as the engine pulled itself and the train onward through the valley. The coal cars trailed behind as far as he could see. The forward cars were empty and would be left behind on various sidings. The train would probably stop at Mine #2 today.

He glanced at Mary and the others, and then to the creaking, groaning wheels of the heavy, coal-filled cars on the track. When the next car ladder was even with him, he broke into a run, and easily matching the train's slow pace, pulled himself onto the ladder. He could hear Mary shouting at him, but couldn't make out what she was saying for the noise of the train.

"See you at school," he shouted back, laughing, but stopped as he nearly lost his footing on the slippery, frost-covered rungs of the steel ladder. Frightened then for a moment, and white-faced, he held tightly to the cold steel bars. But all was well again. He couldn't let Mary see that he was scared, that riding the train to school was as dangerous as she had said. The older kids did it all the time.

He leaned out, holding on to one of the top rungs, and waved to his sisters and younger brother in the distance. "Look," he shouted, laughing. He held one leg out straight, dangling it in the air as he waved.

Then came the jolt. They found out later that a wagon was stuck on the tracks. The rapid banging of coupling to coupling came back from the engine. The heavy wheels slid, sparking and screeching along the rails. William fell. The square end of a tie hurt his back. He always remembered the blow to his back. But nothing else. The sharp wheels severed his legs at the knees.

When Mary reached him, he was on his back, blood pumping in spurts onto the cinder road bed. Quickly Mary took command. "Get Momma," she cried to Violet, who stood crying several yards away. "Go," she shouted into her face. "Get Momma!"

As Violet turned and sprinted along the track, Mary pushed Richard to the ground and pulled his pants off of him. He too was sobbing. "Don't look," she commanded. She tore the leather belt out of its loops and moved to William. She tied the belt tightly around one leg. With the trousers she tied off the other leg. She looked into William's face. His mouth hung open. There was no expression at all on his face; it was blank, as if all his being was moving to control or protect in some way this cruel change in his body, and Mary thought her little brother was dead. The flow of blood slowed. Cinders stuck to the bits of jagged flesh surrounding the shattered bones of his leg.

A couple of other children came running along the path. "Help me!" she cried as she saw the Hatfield boy approaching. "Help me get him home."

The boy looked, then ran to the side of the right-of-way. He vomited into the bushes. That done, he ran to Mary. He picked William up and hoisted him onto his shoulder. He ran and Mary followed. Richard fell down beside her. She lifted him into her arms. It seemed forever until she heard the horses. Robert came first, on the workhorse, bareback, kicking the horse's already heaving sides. Behind him came Thomas. Robert sped past them. Mary caught up with the Hatfield boy as he was lifting William up to his father. Then William was lying across the horse before Thomas. The horse wheeled and was gone.

And then there was nothing. She and Richard and the other children, the Hatfield boy looking dumbly at the hillside, blood covering him completely, milled around in confusion. She sat down in exhaustion with Richard still in her arms as it all caught up with her.

Robert pushed the horse as fast as it would go. On he rode, shouting to the occasional groups of children making their way to school to get out of the way. And then he was there and at the medical building. The door was locked, but he knew that the doctor stayed in the apartment in the back of the building. He pounded on the door until he heard the voice growling from within: "All right. All right. I'm coming." The door opened, and the doctor stood blinking into the morning light.

"Get your bag and come with me," Robert commanded.

"Now wait a minute, young man," the doctor said, rubbing his eyes. "What's the trouble?"

"My brother's legs are cut off."

"In the mine?" the doctor asked as he pulled a coat on.

"Get your bag and come on."

The man opened a cabinet door and pulled the heavy, leather bag from a shelf within.

"What mine is he at?"

"Just past Mine #3."

"Do you live in the camp?" he asked, stopping in the middle of the room.

"No."

A frown came over the man's face. "Surely you understand …."

Robert reached in his pocket, pulled out his knife, and extended the razor-sharp blade. "You come. Right now," he said in a whisper, barely able to speak through the lump in his throat.

"Put that away. I'm coming."

By the time Robert and the doctor reached the Greene cabin, Gertrude had gotten the bleeding stopped. She had replaced the crude tourniquets that Mary had applied with leather straps cut from deerskin. William regained consciousness only when Gertrude began washing the bloody stumps. She applied salt water, dissolving pickling salt into the pot of tea that was her daily luxury and drizzling the mixture over the bloody flesh, then bandaged them with soft cotton cloth from one of Mary's dresses. William's screaming while she worked on his legs hurt her, but she was glad for it. She could believe he would live.

The doctor inspected her work, and aside from giving William a shot of morphine, declared that all that was possible had been done. The bleeding had been the main problem, and Mary had taken the steps that had saved her brother's life. The doctor told Gertrude to give the boy whiskey or marijuana tea, or whatever she had on hand for pain as he needed it.

Thomas had waited outside after helping Gertrude wash the stumps and bandage them. Williams's piercing cries had cut through any illusions he held about his life here. He stood beside the porch, looking down over the gray valley, which in reality was gray from the burning slag heap at the mine. It had been burning for a week now, billowing its sulfurous fumes and residue over the river and the valley beyond. The coal train still sat immobile on the track below.

Thomas saw the world as dim and shapeless at this moment. He felt nothing. He gazed at an object, but saw through it and beyond. At first the thoughts had raced through his mind as he helped Gertrude tend to their son. He would blow up the railroad. He would destroy the mine. He would kill Harris. But he quickly realized, these murderous thoughts crowding against his sorrow, that the men who needed killed in this world are always in hiding, cowards that they are, and cannot be reached. Now he felt nothing. Subdued and silent, he didn't even hear the doctor step onto the porch. Robert came out with him.

They came over to Thomas. "He's going to be all right. Let me give you the name of a doctor in Huntington you can take him to in a couple of months when his legs have begun to heal. It's expensive, but this doctor can make a pair of legs for him. He'll be able to walk again." The doctor set his bag on the porch, took out a pencil and paper, and scribbled a name and address. Thomas took it without speaking.

Robert stood beside them. "Doctor," he started. The unshaven, hastily dressed man turned toward him. "What I done. I didn't know what I was doing."

The doctor put his arm on Robert's shoulder as they turned away. Thomas stood as before, gazing out over the valley and the steep mountain wall across the river. "You were right," the doctor said. "I can't blame you for what you did. It's a damn fool thing, me being a doctor and having somebody tell me who I can treat and who I can't.

You tell your ma I'll come back up to check for infection in a couple of days."

The doctor turned and started to his horse. "Wait a minute. We didn't ... how much do we owe you?"

The doctor got on the horse and reined it down the slope, ignoring Robert's question.

Thomas had buried plenty of people before, but never a pair of legs. The day remained overcast, adding to Thomas's building depression. He carried William's legs up the slope. They were heavy. He inspected the sharp bones protruding from the ends and cringed, every nerve in his body feeling what it must be like for his son who lay in the cabin. He stood for some time, a leg in each hand, trying to decide where to bury them. Suddenly he knew that it didn't matter. The earth would know what to do with them wherever he laid them. Robert carried the shovel and followed his father to the chosen spot at the base of the mountain and Thomas dug a deep cylindrical hole and dropped the legs within.

Chapter Seven

Thomas pulled the crumpled paper from his pocket and looked at it again. Dr. Cain. Huntington. What would it cost to take William there? He only knew they wouldn't be able to afford it, not unless they sold the farm. He put the paper back in his pocket and walked through the still-unplanted garden plot toward the cabin.

When he reached the front porch, Mary was giving William one of her schoolbooks and instructing him in the next day's assignments. The boy's pant legs hung limply over the edge of his chair. He had taken it well, losing his legs. "They ain't there no more, and that's that," he had told Thomas a few days earlier. "Everybody quit acting like I'm some sort of a cripple, 'cause I ain't. Soon's I learn how to use these crutches a little better, I'll be all right."

Thomas retraced his steps back around the cabin and through the garden. He kept on going toward the mine. That morning Hutch, who had replaced Dawson as mine operator, had told him to come back later in the day, when he would be free to talk.

The guard at the east gate to the camp let Thomas in after he found out his business. In the distance, the street was filled with children, outdoors after their day at school. Hutch was in his office.

Thomas had learned to be as blunt as Hutch whenever he talked to him. "What are you paying per acre?" Thomas asked.

Hutch frowned and pushed his chair away from the desk. "You ready to sell?"

"Maybe."

"Six dollars an acre."

"Last time you were over it was seven dollars."

"Times are changing."

"Forget it then. There are lots of companies trying to buy land. I'm going to get ten dollars an acre when I sell. The timber alone is worth ten times that." Thomas turned and started for the door.

"Wait a minute, dammit," Hutch shouted. "Just tryin' to bargain with you a little." He studied the pile of paperwork on his desk for a moment, then said, "I think we can pay it. I'll have to see if Harris wants to pay that much."

"He will," Thomas said. "I'll be ready to sell about a hundred acres in a few weeks. The mountainside—that's all I'll sell. I'll be keeping my bottomland." And Thomas turned and walked out of the office. He heard Hutch shout something after him, but he kept on going. He knew if Hutch wouldn't pay top price, a land company would as an investment. There had been plenty of company representatives through the valley trying to buy his land. They knew the property next to any of the active mines was worth a lot. And so did Thomas.

That night Thomas wrote a letter to Dr. Cain in Huntington. In a couple of weeks he received an answer. The doctor explained that a couple of surgeries on William's legs would be necessary before he could fit him for artificial limbs. And the doctor, though sympathetic about the boy's plight, set the cost at six hundred dollars for everything.

Thomas had already made his decision when nightfall saw the family gathered before the fireplace. Gertrude and Thomas had not discussed the possibility of moving from the valley since before William's accident.

Richard had just finished his painful, nightly ritual of washing himself at the artesian well, and was putting on his shivering act before the hearth. "We're going to move," Thomas said.

A silence overtook the room. A locust log popped in the fireplace and another shifted, sending a spray of sparks up the chimney.

Violet was the first to speak. "But where?"

Robert spoke out defiantly, "I ain't going."

Thomas looked at this version of himself, the tall, muscular young man's shadow pasted against the wall by the flickering light of fire. "We'll deal with that later, Robert. You will be coming. We need you."

"You got to come," Mary told him.

A great, sudden calm filled Gertrude. Finally, she thought. Finally he sees.

"What will happen to the farm?" James asked.

"Matthew is getting married this summer, you know. I've already talked to him. He was planning on building a house on your grandpa's land, but he like the idea of taking over our place and the farm when we leave. I'm going to have to sell some of the land. Probably a hundred acres."

"You can't," Robert said.

"We have to," Thomas answered. "I won't sell it all. We'll still have the bottomland. No matter what happens to us after we leave here, we'll always have this farm. We'll always know that we can come here. But it's time for us to go."

"Where are we going?" Gertrude asked, wondering if Thomas had already planned everything without talking to her about it.

"I've read a lot about Williamson in the newspapers. There's a big rail yard there. I can probably get a job there. Or maybe we can start a business of our own after a while. Maybe a grocery. Folks always need food." Thomas spoke deliberately, confidently. The decision was made. They had to talk about it and plan it now. "But I'm not sure if there's a high school there. If there isn't, we'll probably have to move to Huntington, maybe even Ohio."

"I don't want to go," James said.

"You can stay here with me," Robert joined in again.

"Don't keep talking nonsense," Thomas said sternly. "We're all going. We're sticking together. There's nothing more important than the family. You're all going to go to high school."

Gertrude was elated. Her dreams for her children were going to come true. At least they would have a chance beyond the mining camps, a chance to leave the slag heaps and fighting behind.

Thomas continued. "There's lots of reasons why we are leaving here. Things I don't expect you to understand. But your mother's been right all along, insisting that you get all the education you can. There's only one reason that the coal companies have been able to gain control of the land here—their people have more education. They're no smarter; they've just been exposed to things that folks around here never knew existed."

The room was quiet for a moment. It was dark except for the light from the fire, and Mary rose to light one of the oil lamps hanging beside the doorway.

"Once you're educated you can choose your own path. You can return here if you want. We'll still have this bit of bottomland. You can farm. You can do anything you want with your lives. But for now it's my decision and your mother's as to what's best for the family. The decision is made. Everyone will help."

They talked late into the night, making vague plans that had no real substance, but which would help them prepare themselves mentally for what lay ahead. Mary was the most excited about their plans. She would live in a city! Thomas took Robert and James aside and told them he was going to need their help more than ever, more than on the farm even, and that they had to cooperate with him in every way.

"But I can't go to high school," Robert told his father. "I'm sixteen years old. I'm too old to be goin' to school."

"You're going to try it. For a year at least. After that, if you don't like it, you can get a job or do whatever you want."

Thomas set about getting ready to leave his valley. Once the decision was made, he put all his energy into preparations. The immediate goal was for him to find a job, and then a house for the family. Matthew would take care of the planting for this year.

A few days later, Hutch told Thomas that Harris would take the land at ten dollars an acre. Thomas would keep the fields. They weren't yet certain of the acreage, but until the surveying could be done, Thomas demanded a one hundred dollar deposit, which Hutch reluctantly paid him.

A couple of days after the land sale was agreed upon, Thomas hitched a ride on the caboose of one of the coal trains. By evening he was in Williamson.

He had been in Williamson once before, when he had tried logging one year, riding the logs through the swift Tug to the more placid Sandy

River. Then there had been only about fifteen houses strung out along the railroad. But now! What a change had occurred. There were hundreds of houses, a huge railroad yard that handled the coal coming out of the southern fields, a waterworks, and electric light poles along the main street. Various industries filled the land along the railroad. He was amazed and confused by these changes, but set his mind on his task.

Thomas checked into the N&W Hotel. He would stay there tonight and find out about jobs in the area and about schooling. The schooling was the most important thing.

As he left his room later to look for a place to get dinner, he felt as if he were in some new world. It simply couldn't have happened, Thomas told himself as he gazed around at the electric lighting and busy street. It was too fast.

A couple of doors down from the hotel was Hoyt's Saloon. He sat down at the dark, wood bar and ordered a ham sandwich and a beer.

As he paid the bartender a few minutes later, Thomas asked him how jobs were.

"Railroad's been hirin'. Everybody is. If you can stand up by yourself you can get work here. I ain't got time to talk now. Too busy." The bartender pointed out a heavyset man sitting by himself at one of the tables. "Talk to that feller. John Long's his name. He's just waiting for a card game to come along. He'll tell you all you need to know. He always seems to know something about everybody's business."

Thomas finished his sandwich, got a refill on his beer, and walked over to the table. Before he could even introduce himself, the man invited him to sit down.

"Play cards?"

"What? No," Thomas said. "Used to a little."

"Just getting' ready to deal a few hands when the boys get here. Never too many in a card game."

"Maybe next time around. The bartender said maybe you could help me. I need information about the town here. School and jobs and all."

"Need a job? If I was looking I think I'd go on the railroad. Ain't bad if you can get on as a brakeman or conductor. Make the most money and do the least work. Course you got to be able to read and pass the test they give you. Don't know why exactly. Don't take no brains to ride a train."

"They're hiring now?"

"Couple days ago they was. Goes in spells, though. They been going like crazy all this year. Nothin' but coal. You dig coal or you work for the railroad. Couple of new industries in town, though."

"Is there a high school in town?"

"Well now, that's one thing we ain't got. I heard tell one of the churches has a school in their basement. Been a lot of talk about building one. Just talk so far. I suspect in a few years they'll finally get one built. What you wanting one of them for? You a school teacher?"

"No. For my children."

"You're serious, ain't you?" the stout man asked.

"Yes."

"Well, I'd side with you. We need a school bad. But so far the mayor ain't had enough gumption to make these coal companies and railroads pay their taxes. Hell, old Sid there," and he nodded toward the bartender, "he pays as much tax on his little garden patch up the holler as some of these coal mines. It ain't just the mayor, though. It's mainly them county commissioners. They didn't build them big houses they live in on just their county salaries. Everybody knows it, but they don't seem to care as long as they got jobs …. Besides, not many folks got any schoolin' around here, and they're making out all right."

Thomas had learned what he needed to know. When several men came in a few minutes later, Thomas thanked John Long and stood up to make room for the newcomers.

"Sure you won't join us now? We can pull another chair up here and deal you in. Can't lose any money with these cheapskates. Nickel limit."

"Appreciate the offer. Maybe some other time."

In the morning Thomas bought a train ticket to Huntington. By noon he was in the great city. He hardly knew where to begin, but he did know that this, or a place like it, was where the family would have to live if the children were to go to high school.

He felt out of place at the depot in his rough clothes. For the first time ever, he realized that he was poorly dressed.

He felt even more out of place in the clothing store he entered after walking several blocks. The clerk regarded him coolly, as if he were an intruder to this world of finery, which indeed he was.

"May I help you , sir?"

"I'd like to buy a suit."

"How much do you want to spend, sir?"

How much did he want to spend? The question struck him funny. Strange that a man could spend varying amounts of money to cover his body in an acceptable manner. It made no sense. "What's the cheapest thing you got?"

"Well, sir. Follow me if you will." The clerk made his way along the aisle. Quickly he took Thomas's chest measurements. "Forty-six," he said and rummaged through a rack of hanging suits of solid-colored, burlap-like material. Thomas felt the material of the suits. Heavy and durable.

"How much are these?" Thomas asked.

"Sixteen dollars."

"What's the next cheapest?"

"Twenty-five dollars."

"Let me take a look at those."

The clerk led him up the narrow aisle past a three-sided mirror. Thomas felt a couple of the pin-striped and herringbone-patterned suits. The material felt thin and cheesy to him. Thomas started laughing.

"What is it, sir?"

"These suits wouldn't last half as long as your cheap ones," he said. "Why are these more expensive?"

"Well, sir," the clerk started, and looked sidelong at Thomas as he pulled a coat sleeve out for inspection. "It's the patterns and the fine texture of the cloth."

Thomas started back for the cheaper suits. "Have you got one of these to fit me?" he asked when the clerk caught up with him.

"Yes, sir. There's one in your size. This brown one," he said as he picked the suit off the rack.

"Where do I put it on?"

The clerk pointed out a small passageway behind a thick, velvety curtain.

Thomas came back out in a few minutes wearing the pants. He carried the coat over his arm. "Tell you what. It fits all right. You get these pant legs sewed up right quick, and I'll take it."

"If you could leave it, sir …."

"No, I'll wait."

In a half hour Thomas was on his way, looking like a different man with his suit and tie.

His muscular frame filled the suit coat perfectly, though the pants were loose at the waist.

He still didn't know where he was going. Down the block he saw a policeman walking along the storefronts. Thomas approached him. "Afternoon," the policeman said as Thomas stopped before him.

"Afternoon," Thomas greeted him. "I'm trying to find my way around. I thought maybe you could help me."

"Be glad to."

"Where's the high school located?"

"There's two of them. One is about twenty blocks to the east. The other is over on the west side."

Thomas was puzzled. Two high schools!

"I would say the one you want is on the west side."

Thomas also got directions to Dr. Cain's office; it was in the downtown area and only a couple of blocks from where he was now. Then he was on his way again, still at a loss as to what he should do. He couldn't wander around the streets all day.

The May sun was hot and bright as it cascaded from the cement and steel fixtures along the city street. Thomas was sweaty and uncomfortable in his new suit, and had loosened his tie and the top button of his shirt by the time he reached the doctor's office.

He stepped into the outer room, and as several people seated in the carpeted room turned to stare at him, he was not even sure why he was here. He had come on an impulse, trusting to the usual intelligence and education of the few doctors ever in his valley. He had never yet met a totally dishonest and stupid doctor.

The thin, wooden door protecting the nurse's cubbyhole slid open suddenly, and a middle-aged woman in white was looking at him. He walked over to the window and explained that he would like to see the doctor about his son's condition, and that he would make an appointment after he had spoken to the doctor. She frowned and hesitated.

"I've come a long way. I'll just take a minute of his time."

"If you don't mind waiting, I think you can see him. It might be an hour or two."

Thomas nodded and took a seat on one of the soft chairs.

The room was still and quiet. The rustling dress of the woman next to him broke the stillness now and then, along with an occasional cough. A gray-looking man with an arm missing sat staring blankly at a picture of a horse on the wall. Thomas imagined himself sitting on the porch of his cabin, looking out over the valley. He could hear the quail whistling their distinct melodies at sunset, the raucous cries of the blue jay that had taken up residence in one of the pines before the cabin, the chattering of squirrels. How superior the sounds in his mind seemed to the starched, muffled sounds in this tiny room. But he would become a part of it. His mind was made up. He would learn to live in this city. He had a purpose and could not let that purpose be distorted by his feelings.

When his time came to see the doctor, he followed the nurse along a whitewashed corridor to a small library at its end. The doctor stood up when Thomas entered. "I remember your letter, Mr. Greene," the doctor said as he extended his hand. "Unfortunate for your son. How has he taken it?"

"Real well," Thomas said. "It's hurt him, though. He puts up a good front, but every once in a while it hits him pretty hard."

"Sounds like he's got the courage to overcome his handicap. That's the main thing. That and a lot of encouragement from you. Well, what can I do for you? I understand that your son is not with you today."

"No, I ... I'm moving my family to the city here, and I ... you're the only person I've had any contact with. I learned that I was near your office, so I thought maybe you could steer me in the right direction."

"I'll be glad to help you if I can."

"The reason we're moving here is for the education for my children. The only opportunity where we are now is coal mining, and to my mind that's no opportunity."

"Don't you want to move?"

"Yes. Now we do. It's hard to explain … all the changes that have occurred in only a few years in our area."

"I remember your address listed Matewan for mail delivery. South of Williamson, in the coalfields."

"Yes."

"What in the hell is going on down there?" the doctor asked. "I hear all sorts of stories. And the newspapers. My God. People murdered. What do the miners want?"

"It's not the miners. You wouldn't say that if you saw what was happening."

The doctor studied Thomas's face. "I suppose you're right. Never believe anything until you've seen for yourself if you want to find the truth. Well, it will all come out in the end. 'Mountaineers are always free.'"

Thomas looked quizzically at the doctor.

"State motto," he explained. "You've never heard that?"

"I guess I've said something like it many times."

The nurse tapped on the wood door and entered, depositing a stack of folders before the doctor.

Dr. Cain pointed to the stack and smiled. "Well, I've still got lots to tend to today. What could I help you with?"

"I need to find a job and a house for my family."

"Well, maybe I can be of some help. I know a few people around town. What sort of work do you do?"

"I can do anything, I guess. I thought about the railroad. Brakeman, maybe. I want to do the best-paying sort of work I can find."

"Don't we all," the doctor said, took out his prescription pad, and wrote down a man's name and a brief note. "I've talked to the man who does the hiring for the railroad. He's referred several injured men to me for medical attention. Blair Turner's his name. This might do you some good," he said and gave the note to Thomas.

"Thank you."

"Housing," the doctor said and looked at his watch. Again he scribbled something on his pad and gave it to Thomas. There were several street names on the small square of paper.

"Right in that area is a good family neighborhood. It's close to the grade school. About a mile to the high school." The doctor stood up, and they shook hands again. "Good luck, Mr. Greene. And get your boy in here as soon as you are settled in. You can pay me a little at a time. He's going to be eager to get around, this fine weather keeps up."

"Thank you," Thomas said. "You've been right helpful. Thank you very much."

He needed a job before he could look for a house, and as it was too late in the day to get back to the railroad depot, Thomas checked into a downtown hotel. His room was on the second story facing the street. He sat for a while in a cane-backed chair near the window. The room was done in dark brown paper, shiny, like oilcloth. A pitcher and bowl sat on an oak dresser beside the bed. After a while, used to the room, Thomas began to sense a sort of humming noise around him. He looked around the room for the source and then out the window. There was activity everywhere he could see, people hurrying about, a trolley car banging its way along, a horse and cart rounding the corner. Later, in the middle of the night, Thomas woke to hear the warning bells of a barge on the river. He lay for some time then, thinking ahead to the coming day. Before he drifted off to sleep, he could hear the humming noise again.

In the morning Thomas set off for the depot. He reached Blair Turner's office before anyone was there. He waited on a bench in the marble-floored hallway for an hour until the offices began to come to life. By the time Blair Turner reached his office, there were a dozen men waiting to see him.

"Coming through," Turner said matter-of-factly as he brushed past the group. They filed into his office after him. Turner laid a stack of job applications on his desk and motioned for each man to take one.

"If you can't read or write, get somebody to help you fill it out," Turner said as he plugged in a hot plate behind his desk and set about preparing a pot of coffee.

By the time Thomas had helped a couple of other men fill out their applications and had finished his own, most of the men were already gone, hired or dismissed for one reason or another. A couple of them had been sent to another room to take the test for trainmen. Thomas handed Turner his application along with the note from Dr. Cain.

Turner looked at them, then told Thomas where to go to take his test.

In a few minutes Thomas had completed the test, which was mainly for reading ability. The other men were sitting around the room smoking and talking, awaiting the outcome of the test. "A year ago," one of the men was saying, "my uncle got on. He makes twice what I do down at the mill. It don't make much sense working all day and only making half what another man makes."

"It sure don't. But what you going to do? You can't do nothin' but try to get where the money is."

The door adjoining Turner's office was opened and Turner stood looking at the men, a bundle of papers in his hands.

"Greene," he said and motioned for Thomas to enter his office. "The rest of you can go."

Thomas stood up and walked around the table. "Wonder who the hell he knows," one of them said.

"We don't see many perfect scores on these tests," Turner told Thomas as they sat down. "Not because of the test. It's simple enough. We'll probably move you up to conductor if you work out all right at brakeman. Need smart men to run the train, make sure all the paperwork gets done right. The conductor gets paid a little more too. If you stay clean and follow orders, you'll make out all right."

Thomas explained that he had to move his family to Huntington before he could start work. Turner said he could start in a week. "But not a day longer than a week. I need men today."

That afternoon, after finally finding half a house on a tree-lined street, it all began to catch up with Thomas. He was tired, but he had no home to go to, just this busy city swirling around him, its thousands of people scurrying to get wherever they were going by a certain time, the trolley cars clanking by him. Thomas felt dizzy as he walked back to the depot. Everywhere people and machines.

As he boarded the evening train for Williamson an hour later, his thoughts were of his home in the mountains. His valley. It had seemed like it was his once. But he forced himself to concentrate on the planning before him. The next week would be hectic, but he knew that the sooner they were settled into their house, the better off they would all be. They couldn't bring many of their belongings with them. Nearly everything that the Greene family owned, and which they had made over the years to make their lives comfortable in their mountain environment, would be useless here.

Thomas was glad that Robert and James were old enough to help him. They would have to build the furniture once they got moved here. Robert could take charge of that. Thomas would have to buy many of the things they would need here—the stove, icebox, clothes, bedding, everything nearly. But he had a good job. That would help them through the first year. And he would have the money from the land he was selling. Strange, he thought, that the same force that was destroying the mountains was giving him the money he needed to move on, to escape. He didn't know what that meant.

A good job. That made all the difference in the world now. On the farm they could live well by working hard. Here in the city one lived well by getting a good job or becoming something—a brakeman, storekeeper, skilled craftsman, a doctor or lawyer. Whatever one became determined how he could live. Those who weren't educated enough to become skilled workers or professionals were left behind. The neighborhoods of the city explained the structure as well as anything. Thomas had already noticed the many different areas—nice homes faded into unpainted homes, which faded into shacks. The riverfront. The downtown area. The industrial sections. The residential neighborhoods. The outlying mansion-dominated estates. It was a cruel system, he could see, a system controlled by a select minority. But for the doctor, he might now be combing the riverfront for some menial job. The family might be moving to some grimy tenement beneath the shadow of one of the smoke-belching factories.

As the train left the sprawling city behind that evening, a nausea overcame Thomas. But only for a few moments. Wherever he went, wherever he was forced to go in this city, and whatever he was forced into, Thomas Greene would seek the best that was available for his family.

Chapter Eight
1919

It was one of those rare November days that would have one believe that it is not really November at all, but the middle of September or early October. It was sunny and dry, with a warm wind sending leaves rattling along the ground, tumbling and bumping until they should break their brittle selves to pieces, or land impacted upon the millions of others caught in fences or ditches, or entwined, as in a spider's web, in the long grass that had grown since the last mowing.

The Armistice Day parade had reached its destination, and soldiers and bandsmen were breaking ranks and seeking out family or remembrances of family throughout the cemetery. Colorful wreaths had been placed by the veterans' organizations on the simple headstones of the fallen soldiers. The war had been over for a year now, and though the country celebrated its victory, Gertrude could not think of the war or her Robert without tears forming.

Gertrude said a prayer as she knelt before the headstone and placed an arrangement of dried flowers before her oldest son's marker. Robert's body was not here, but she had to believe that his spirit was. It was a strange and sad thing to her that the one child who had remained farthest from her, the one whom she had not been able to reach, and who had not shared her dreams, would be the first to be taken from her.

With Richard and Thomas on either side of her, Gertrude stood up and turned away from the grave. They started back for the highway, where the bus would stop and pick them up for the return to town and the home that they had all helped build in 1905.

Time had passed cruelly in its swiftness for Gertrude and had scattered all her children but this one brooding, young man who walked beside her. Her dreams for her children had come true—all of them had graduated from high school and several from college. She needed only to imagine the farm and valley, the picture of which had been renewed and altered in her mind over the years by visits there, to know that coming here to Huntington had been the best thing she and Thomas could ever have done for the children.

The valley and mountains of her childhood had been left behind by the rest of the world. The farm was more isolated than ever. There was no school nearby any longer. What the mining industry had first built up, it had just as quickly torn down. All was chaos now. New mines opened, and the old ones that were not yet worked out were closed. Old mines filled with water as it became more expensive for the operators to get at the coal; it was cheaper to close the old mine and dig a new hole into the mountain somewhere else.

She glanced at Thomas at her side. What was it that kept him from showing the signs of age? She felt with pride the muscular arm coupled with hers. His prominent features were not marred by the wrinkles that beset most men his age. She loved him still. He had never balked at the task of raising the children in the city. Her dream had, over the years, become his dream. As he rose at midnight, or two or four in the morning, to take the call to be at the depot for a run to Charleston, or Williamson, or Logan, or wherever he was assigned, a trip that would take him away from his family for days at a time, there was always a purpose behind what he was doing, a purpose that had enabled him to overcome his feelings about the land that had been, in a sense, been taken from him. He had always had a purpose. Whatever he did was carefully deliberated between his mind and feelings. When he found no reason to disregard his feelings, he followed them. When the mind calculated the feelings to be in error, he followed his mind.

As they waited with scores of others beside the busy highway for the urban bus, Gertrude was glad for the two strong men beside her. Soon Richard would also be setting out on his own in marriage, and Gertrude already felt as if she had a new daughter. There was more happiness than sadness in her life.

All of her children had gone their ways through the years. And she could think of their accomplishments with pride through the moments of sadness that beset her at some remembrance of each of them, of a time when they had needed her. They had all seemed to inherit the strong-willed drive and sense of purpose of their father. All except Robert. What had he done and seen that had limited his vision, that had made him return to the coalfields to be battered and abused by the barons of the mountains, the coal operators? She would never understand that. Even after he was blacklisted from gaining employment in the mines, with a long scar, received at the hands of strikebreaker, running from his cheekbone to his mouth in a curving, purple line, he had joined the Army to serve his country.

But while she mourned for the shortened life of her firstborn, there remained the courageous progress of the others, who had taken to their education as she had dreamed that they would. James, a high school science teacher, lived in Columbus, Ohio, with his wife and three children. Mary had also become a teacher. She had taught in Huntington before marrying the aggressive hardware salesman and moving to Charleston with him.

And William. His blustering self-confidence about the loss of his legs had gradually given way to his fears. It had been difficult for him to get to and from school each day, and he had begun to realize the severe limitations that had been imposed upon him for the rest of his life. But there came a day when he overcame his fears and regained his confidence in himself. He was still using his crutches, trying to get used to his new wooden legs during his first winter here. Twelve years old. He and James were coming home after school when three of their classmates began teasing him, calling him peg leg and mimicking him in their childish ignorance. James took on all three boys after one of them tripped William. He lay on the pavement, watching as James began to take a beating on his behalf. He stood up then and hit the first boy with his hickory-wood crutch. The other one, the boy who had held James from behind, he gave a sharp rap in the kidney and then jumped on him, wrestling him to a tie. The family always remembered the story; it exemplified William. He could do just about anything he needed to do or set his mind on doing, and what he had ultimately set it on was becoming a doctor. He lived in Louisville now. William was the only one besides Richard who had not married. He'd been too busy, or so he said, with his schooling, his recently opened medical practice, and the research he was continually carrying on.

Violet had married a boy she met at the college in Huntington. They lived in Parkersburg now, where her husband had entered his father's growing machine shop business. Thomas had always said jokingly that it was a good thing the boy's father had money.

And Richard had stayed in Huntington and gone to work on the railroad. Richard would be the only one close to her now.

Gertrude's mother had not been well for the last year, and Gertrude had tried to persuade Mary and Gabriel to move to the city to live with her and Thomas. Thomas, knowing Gabriel's mind, had only laughed. And he was right, Gertrude had found; neither Gabriel nor Mary had any inclination to leave their farm and come to the city. So in order to be closer to her folks, she and Thomas had decided to move south to Williamson to be able to help them as they needed it, and to visit them more often. It was nearly an all-day journey to get down to see them from Huntington. Living in Williamson would let them visit more often.

Thomas was looking forward to getting back to the mountains. Of course there were mountains around Huntington, but one didn't live on them. They were simply there, and but for the lack of mountains in the wide valley created over the ages by the Ohio River, there would not have been a city there in the first place. For several years after the children had made their varied ways away from him and Gertrude, Thomas had wanted to get out of the city. But Gertrude seemed contented, so he had dismissed his thoughts.

Thomas knew his way around Williamson by now, having ridden the train there hundreds of times. The previous summer, he had bought a lot in a developing area just outside Williamson, up one

of the many creek hollows that fed into the city, and
had hired a carpenter to build a cottage for them. He
was quitting his railroad job, which kept him away
from Gertrude as much as with her over the last
fifteen years. He and Gertrude were both looking
forward to getting settled into their new home,
which was scheduled to be finished by the end of
November.

Thomas had also lined up a job for himself
in Williamson the last time he had been there. Jobs
were scarcer then he had thought they would be,
and he had finally taken a job with a small company
that manufactured electrically powered coal cars for
use in the mines. He would be running a lathe,
turning down the steel bars that would form the
axles to be used under the cars. He wasn't looking
forward to staying in the smoky, grimy factory
every day, but at least he would have a job that
allowed him to be at home with his wife every
night. That had been his goal, to get work that
would allow him to spend his free time with
Gertrude.

Richard would be able to visit them
frequently in Williamson. The way the trains had
been running, he would see them at least every ten
days. He would stay at their house with them and
could save himself the cost of bed and board while
he was in town.

The children reacted to the news of the
move with surprise. All of them except William. He
wrote them a long letter wishing them happiness in

their new home. He had known all along, he wrote,
that sooner or later they would move from
Huntington. He promised he would be in
Williamson to see them at Christmas.

And then near the end of November,
Thomas and Gertrude were in their new cottage up
the creek hollow. Only a few people had built out
their way so far, and they reveled in the
rediscovered isolation and solitude. They had a
good level area for garden space, and good well
water, almost as good, Thomas said, as the water
from the artesian well on the farm. The mountain
ridge that back-dropped their house and yard was
owned by a land company, but Thomas, like the
other land owners in the area, had obtained a ninety-
nine-year lease on the hillside for only five dollars a
year. He had no fear that there would be any mines
opened along the watershed, not because of a lack
of coal, but because Williamson needed room to
grow. The town was the hub of the coalfields. Here
the coal was routed out of the mountains. Here had
developed the industries that kept the machinery
going, which made and repaired the coal-digging
equipment. Here the executives of the coal and
railroad concerns could get comfortable lodging,
take the train to the sites of their investments, and
be back in Williamson the same day. It had become
dangerous, or so they thought, for certain of them to
be away from the protection of the city overnight.

The bitterness that had started with the
coming of the mines many years before had grown.

There would be peace in the fields for a while, then the operators would have a bad market and pass the loss of profit on to the miners, and the trouble would be renewed. Over the years there had grown a sizeable mass of men, biding their time, waiting for revenge, for justice for themselves, their fathers, and their children. These angry men lived as best they could in the mountains, scrounging for work in or out of the mines, or moved to the cities to become part of the mass of displaced humanity that provided the labor for industry.

Thomas grew used to his job at the factory, or rather, he resigned himself to spending ten hours a day there. He did his work, did it correctly and efficiently, and learned to ignore his personal feelings while he was there. But as with his job on the railroad, he could never escape the feeling that what he was doing was somehow artificial work— that he was only involved in some sort of game designed by he knew not whom.

Two days before Christmas, Thomas met William at the depot in Williamson. As William stepped from the passenger car into the early darkness of a winter evening, supporting himself with the cane that had become an inseparable part of him through the years, Thomas left the two men with whom he had been talking and rushed to meet him. William stood in the fine crystal snow that had just started falling, dropped his suitcase and medical bag on the wood-plank loading platform and watched as his father approached.

"You're looking good," Thomas said as they embraced.

"If I look as good as you when I get to be an old man, then I'll say I look good."

"Old man," Thomas laughed. "Watch who you call an old man! It's a good thing you carry that stick."

"It's good to see you. How's Mother?"

"Well. And happy."

Thomas picked up the grip that William had set on the platform. William picked up the black valise, and they moved toward the depot. "Do you always carry your medical bag with you?" Thomas asked as he held the door.

"Everywhere I go. Never know when I'll need it."

The two men Thomas had been talking to were sitting by the coal-fired stove in the corner of the room. They stood up as Thomas and William approached, and Thomas introduced William to them.

"Pleased to meet you," one of them said. "I've heard so much about you, I was beginnin' to wonder if you was real or just a story your old man made up."

"You don't want to believe too much of it. Never believe a man when he's talking about his children."

"Like some coffee?" the other asked him.

"Never touch the stuff. Now if you had a snort of something a little stronger ...."

The man held up his hand to silence William and pulled a flask from the top pocket of his overalls. They passed it around.

Thomas explained that the men, friends of his from when he worked on the railroad, were making a run along the Tug River in the morning. He and William and Gertrude would be riding on the caboose with them down to Gabriel's and Mary's farm for Christmas. William's face lit up with a surprise at the news. "Good," he said. "It'll be good to see them again."

"Look at that," one of the men said and nudged Thomas. "You get him down in the hills far enough, you might never get him back out."

Thomas and William took their leave, and in a short while had left the electric, coal-powered brightness of the city behind them.

Gertrude had been waiting for them before the hearth. When she heard the door latch, she rushed to meet them. The reunion was a tearful one for Gertrude. She hadn't seen William for over a year now. There was a special bond between her and this child that she had helped make the journey from weakness to strength.

They sat and she served the stew she had been keeping hot for their supper. They talked for a while of the family. Letters had become less frequent as the years passed, and now not many of the family members even knew what the others

were like or what they were doing. Thomas knew
that this estrangement was the price of their success,
knew it instinctively when they had left the Tug
Valley, and he would not have wanted it to be
otherwise. The tidal wave of ugliness that the one-
industry culture of the mines had foisted upon he
and his wife and children was something that they
had needed to escape. After a while, the talk
between Thomas and William turned to the miners'
struggle.

William sat shaking his head as he learned
of the latest atrocities in the warlike coalfields. "It's
strange knowing what's really happening here, then
seeing the newspapers distort it all, so that folks
believe the miners are a bunch of Communists
trying to wreck our government. Nobody knows
what's going on. I don't have the time to read the
magazines to understand all of it."

"Over near Logan, there's a tent camp where
the men have been going when they get evicted
from their homes," Thomas said. "Right now
they're sitting out there in some field freezing, and
trying to scrounge enough food to feed their
families. It's not right. The feelings are bad, really
bad. It's going to blow up. Too many men have
been hurt now. But they're up against a regular
army. The sheriff over in Logan County, name's
Don Chafin, he's got a couple hundred men who'll
take up arms with him. Got this siren in Logan they
blow when trouble breaks out. The mine companies
have hired hundreds of these Baldwin-Felts

detectives. Gunslingers is what they are. Lots of outsiders. They all coming running when there's trouble."

William sat listening. "I've seen ads in the papers asking for money for the miners on strike. United Mine Workers."

"They haven't been able to organize here yet. Up in the Kanawha Valley they've made some headway since the war. But that's what the operators are fighting here. They don't want unions. With mine camps laid out in the middle of nowhere, you know how it is, it's next to impossible to get any organization going. Trouble breaks out, no one even hears about it for a couple of days. And then there's nothing to be done. The sheriff and his thugs are always there first."

"It would be cheaper to give the men what they want instead of paying all these gunmen."

"That's the truth. And from all I've heard, they pay the strike-breakers more than they pay the miners. Course, it's hard to separate rumors from the truth. But I know what I've seen, what happened near the farm when you were just little."

William sat shaking his head. "It just doesn't make any sense. It's like … like another world down here."

"You two quit getting so worried about things. It's Christmas," Gertrude said.

William stood up and kissed her. "You're right. No more about the mines. It's going to be a good Christmas."

Chapter Nine

It felt strange to Thomas to be going to work back in Williamson the Monday after Christmas.

"When are you coming back home?" Matthew had asked him the day before, as they sat together for their Christmas dinner at Gabriel's cabin.

The question had hit him strangely. Coming home? Where was his home? It was wherever Gertrude was, he knew that much. One's home is where he feels right, where he can escape at least a few of the fears and doubts of being alive. And where was his home? He had told Matthew that he just moved and wasn't about to go through it again. But the thought of returning to his valley to be among the people he had for many years considered to be his family was to remain with him.

The Harris Company had never mined the land that Thomas had sold them. They had opened another mine several years before on the Davis land on which they held title, but aside from clearing the heavy timber from the land he had sold them, they had changed nothing on his land. And there was little chance now that the Harris Company would ever use the mountainside he had sold them. They

had moved out; they were gone. The mine near
Thomas's land had been destroyed a couple of
months before.

"The union men was around quite a lot
then," Gabriel had explained. "They'd get beat up
and come back for more. The folks were plum full
of lies and promises that ain't never been kept. The
operator told the men that there was going to be
another pay cut. That's what finally did it, I guess.
The men had a meeting somewhere that night. Over
on some of Jenkins' land from all I could figure,
away from the guards at the mine."

Most of the men joined the union that night,
Thomas learned. Of course if a man got caught
joining the union, he was fired. The next day when
they went to work, the boss and a dozen of the
guards and deputies met the men.

"One of those guards even had a machine
gun," Gabriel told Thomas in disbelief. "One of the
men was an informer. He was getting paid to keep
an eye on what the rest of the men was doing. I
don't know who the operator was. They've had so
many in the last few years. He started reading off
the men's names who was fired for joining the
union. The men acted real peaceable at first,
couldn't do nothing else with them guards standing
by. So they all went home and acted like they was
packing things up and getting ready to leave. Then
all of a sudden come the shooting. We could hear
that machine gun spittin' and then it quit. Sounded
like a regular war. Then come the dynamitin'. The

miners blew up everything they could. The tipples. Sealed the mines tight. They'll never dig no coal at those mines again. The company just moved out what was left of their machines and closed their store. All the bosses was gone a couple weeks later."

"One of them guards and a couple miners was killed. Only reason I know all this, some of the folks came back and are still living in the mine houses over there. Probably five families left there; they got nowhere to go."

Thomas left the gray skies behind for the gray factory. The walls and ceiling were black from smoke and dirt. The place had a yellowish glint from the grime-covered lights on the high ceiling. He didn't look forward to the coming day's work, standing by the lathe all day, working to make the components to make the cars to haul the coal from the mountain interiors. What did he care about building coal cars? Nothing. He cared nothing for it. The work was meaningless and boring to him.

Thomas went straight to his machine and pushed the starter button. The chuck clunked and turned half a revolution. The smelly cutting oil splashed into the tub under the machine. The electric motor hummed, waiting to begin another day's service.

As Thomas set about sharpening the cutting tool, his thoughts were still of their trip to the valley. He had seen Poland and Barker, the two tenants out of the original three who remained on his land. Poland was glad to see Thomas, who always stopped to visit with him whenever he was there. Though his home had taken on the gray, splintered texture of unpainted wood over the years, it was still his home, and Thomas Greene was largely responsible for its existence.

Gabriel and Thomas and William had gone to the mining camp. They didn't know any of the people there, but after hearing the story of what had happened, William wanted to offer his medical services if any were in need of them.

Thomas thought with pride of his son as he loaded the first bar of cold roll into the machine and tightened the chuck jaws. He set the RPMs down to begin turning the piece when Pete Fawley, the plant superintendent, came by. Pete was stupid, Thomas thought. He was also the son-in-law of the factory owner.

"Mornin', Greene," he said and stopped to watch Thomas work. Thomas always hated it when the man would stand and watch him. Pete was generally friendly enough, but Thomas didn't like him. He was always asking Thomas questions. What did he think about this? And that? "What about those miners?" he asked Thomas one Monday morning shortly after he had taken the job here. "Ain't that something, all the trouble they're causing? Damn Communist agitators."

Thomas had ignored the man's remarks. He had grown used to such talk of equating the miners' unions with the Communists.

The year 1920 worked its way toward summer. All through the southern West Virginia coalfields, miners were striking. The workers had made no headway in their demands for better wages and working conditions and the right to belong to a labor union. Logan County Sheriff Chafin and his company-paid deputies and thugs made sure that the miners did not become union men.

Life had never been valued above independence and justice in these mountains. And it was no different now. Killings were frequent on both sides, but not nearly so frequent as the deaths and injuries inflicted by the unsafe conditions in the mines. A strike might kill one by starvation or a bullet, but the reasoning was that it was better to starve not working than working, and better to risk being shot than being blown to pieces or electrocuted beneath the ground.

The operators' organizations were used to find and make available hundreds of strike-breakers and scabs. And on it went, the union making no headway, the moneyed interests remaining in control. Without organization and money, the miners hadn't a chance. No one seemed to be on their side. No one seemed to know what was happening in the land where the coal to run their generators and motors and trolleys and gadgets was mined. Of if they did know, they didn't care; people competing with each other for jobs and money don't have time to concern themselves.

And the operators seemed not to know what forces they were dealing with in these mountains. Of course, the owners of the mines rarely were in the coalfields anymore. From Pittsburgh or New York City, or wherever the owners lived, they made their decisions. They could not or would not understand that people need the security of a home, be it a cabin on a mountainside or a farm in a valley, or their own home near the mine camp, or that once a man had paid rent on his clapboard house in a mine camp for ten or fifteen years he might have begun to think that it was his own house he was living in. Cut wages, increase production, reduce expenditures, raise prices. The orders came from far away into the coalfields with, as from the start, no acknowledgement of any obligation to the workers.

In late May 1920, the news spread quickly of the gun battle in Matewan in which Sid Hatfield and several other men had taken on the Baldwin-Felts detectives. It was a victory for the miners. Hatfield was the police chief of Matewan. The Baldwin-Felts men were from a Bluefield detective agency that supplied some of the strike-breakers and guns-for-hire for the coalfields. The detectives had just finished evicting a group of miners from their camp homes, a task that Hatfield refused to undertake. Few men could fight the operators on their own terms. Fewer still could stand up to Sid Hatfield, who shot coins out of the air with his forty-five. How it all started remained a mystery, but seven of the feared Baldwin-Felts men were dead, five with bullet holes in their foreheads, and the Matewan Massacre became a story to be told and retold in the tent colonies that sprang up in the mountains.

Richard was on the first train through after the battle. "Folks were quiet but you could see their pride that someone had finally stood up to the Baldwin-Felts men," he told Thomas during a June visit after he was laid off from the railroad. "I've never seen a war up close, but that's what this is."

The tent colonies housed the striking miners, who had, with the help and money of the United Mine Workers, in April struck all of the southern coalfields to settle their grievances once and for all. It made no sense to the southern West Virginia coal miners that they were the only ones in the country not to have the benefits that the union could bring them; they were finished living under the feudal system dictated by the companies. Southern West Virginia had become a battlefield.

Jobs became scarce in Williamson. The train traffic slowed. The empty cars in the yards would stand for weeks at a time until the operators could find enough scabs to resume production. The entire economy slowed to a crawl.

Thomas watched it all without surprise, as if he had known this was all ordained beforehand on the way to the End. Men forced from the land and then from their jobs and then from their homeland could not live. It was that simple. They and their families were starving, with nowhere to go, not a dime in the pocket to buy bread. What had begun only 25 years earlier now had such a head of steam that it could never, to his mind, be arrested. It was the End Times, not populated by black-winged Devils with lolling red tongues but by men in suits and ties buying and selling land and people and getting elected to county and state and federal office. Men stealing from those weaker than themselves. Men acting as corporations, preying on those who could not read or understand the documents used in this thievery and desecration. Soulless men bringing about the End.

A year passed. The strike was still on. The displaced people were starving and being herded here and there by the deputies and gun thugs. Mass warrants were issued for theft or assault or any other charges that could be dreamed up against the men of the tent colonies, and the jails were filled.

But they had made it through the winter without giving up. Everywhere these landless men roamed, helpless yet trying to help themselves the only way they could see to do so—by making the coal companies give them some input into their futures. Spring of 1921 passed and summer wore on, and still the men and the union made no progress. With cold weather not far away, there was no illusion in the minds of these strikers—they could not last out another winter. One way or another, the strike had to be settled.

Late in August came the news that thousands of miners had begun a march from Charleston to Logan. The spark that had ignited their anger was the shooting of Sid Hatfield as he walked up the steps of the courthouse in Welch to stand trial for murder charges from the Matewan Massacre. Several Baldwin-Felts gunmen had shot the unarmed Hatfield.

Rumors flew wildly about the streets of Williamson. Miners from the northern fields were on the march to aid their comrades in the southern fields. They were hell-bent on destroying everything in their path, the stories went. They would be dynamiting any factory or business that did any business with the coal concerns. Thousands of murderers and looters were on the way, first to Logan, then to Williamson.

Thomas Greene was in a depressed state when he left the factory the night he heard of the army of miners, but not because of the rumored march. That was long overdue in his mind. If it took a war to give the miners what they had coming, then let it come, he thought. The plant manager had told Thomas he would have to work late every night so the company could meet the deadlines for a batch of new orders from the northern fields. Times had been hard at the factory since the beginning of the strike the previous year, and for several months they had worked only half days.

The air was crisp as Thomas walked along the railroad right-of-way toward home. A sadness overwhelmed him as he looked up at the full, August moon. He shivered as the cool air descended over him. Was he to spend the rest of his life making axles for coal cars? Time moved so quickly. It seemed to him that his life was being reduced to nothingness. He no longer had a purpose, unless running a lathe could be called a purpose.

His sadness blinded him. It was harvest time. Late August. He would have been cutting the rest of the hay and oats for the livestock now. The corn would be ready in a few more weeks, depending on when it had been planted.

Had it been fifteen years? No. Longer than that. Could he still do it, he asked himself? He tightened his chest and arm muscles into tense, ropy knots. Yes, he would always be able to live from the land. It seemed only yesterday that he had reigned over his land, sat after a day's labors looking out over his valley. He had always worked harder at farming than he did at his job here at the factory. He had been working for himself then. He would feel cheated if he worked that hard at his job here. Like a slave. That's what he was, an industrial slave, he thought. "You'll be staying till eight tonight," his boss told him. Be here at seven. Go home at eight. Be here. Go. Yes sir. Yes, master.

Thomas crossed the tracks and headed for the electric brightness of town. He couldn't go home in such a foul mood.

He ducked down an alley bordering town and entered one of the speakeasies on Third Street. It was smoky and noisy, the working men within drinking, playing cards, and talking, trying to eke some sense or joy out of another day. Thomas sat down at the long bar.

"Well, if it ain't Thomas Greene," chuckled the man next to him. "Never knew you drank."

"Used to try it some. Never was real good at it."

"Well, practice makes perfect. That's what my school teacher always said. Yessir. Practice makes perfect. I been practicin' for over fifteen years, now. Still ain't got the hang of it. What're you drinking?"

"Whiskey," Thomas said. He felt uncomfortable sitting next to this man, Bud Taylor. He worked at the factory where Thomas did. They had seen each other every working day for over two years and had barely spoken a word during that time.

The bartender approached. "Glass of whiskey for my friend here," Bud told him.

"Beer or water with it?" the bartender asked Thomas as he poured the drink.

"Beer," Thomas said and reached for the bills in his pocket.

"I got it," Bud said.

"Thanks."

"Where you from, anyway?" Bud asked thickly.

Thomas looked at Bud, still grimy, as was Thomas, from his day's work. "That's a strange question. I've known you for quite a while and we haven't said a damn thing to each other."

"Hell, I never seen you except at work. No need to get all huffy about it."

Thomas looked at him, then down at his drink. "Bad day."

"Know what you mean. Too long to stay in that stinkin' place." Bud sat for a while, then said, "Something strange about knowing who a man is for two, three years and not know nothin' about him." He gulped the rest of the drink and set the glass loudly on the counter. The bartender came and filled it. Thomas finished his drink and held his glass out. "I got this one," he told Bud.

"But you never come to the bars. That's where you get to know a man. You don't talk much—too damn noisy—when you're working."

"I used to work at something where you'd get to know a man in a day," Thomas said. "Least you'd know what he was like. Now days you don't need to know anybody. It's every man for himself."

Bud stared at the bottles lining the wall before him. "Where'd them days go? A man ain't got time to live anymore." Bud stared ahead as if he were talking to the bottles. "Just ain't got the time to feel alive somehow. I used to feel good. Really good. Course that was when I was a boy, afore I come to town to go to work."

"Didn't you work before you came here?"

Bud looked at Thomas. "You're talking to a hillbilly!" he roared, laughing. "What the hell you mean, didn't I work? When I was eight years old I'd do more work after school than I do all day now." Bud paused and looked at himself in the mirror behind the bottles. He brushed his hair to the side. "I could tell you a story—I will tell you, dammit. Them coal people wonder why folks is strikin' and blowin' up their mines."

"We had this little hillside farm. Wasn't much, I guess. We worked it hard. There was eight of us kids. Wasn't no way but to work it hard. But we lived right. Always plenty to eat. Good eatin', too. Had venison and pork and all the beans and taters a feller'd ever want."

"One day one of them fellers from the coal company come around. I hid in the barn and tried to listen, but I couldn't hear nothin'. Me and Ora was up there. This feller was a'talkin' away and Dad all of a sudden stuck out his jaw, like he done when he was mad, and pointed down the holler. That feller said something else and left. Well, that was the start. We had a bad crop the next year and here come this feller back again. Dad was worried about how we was going to make up what we lost. The rain had ruined most of our corn that year. Dad had been out looking for work but there weren't none. Well that feller stole my Dad's land! Dad sold him the rights to it for fifty cents an acre. Fifty cents an acre! Dad thought it was a good deal, though. He'd got himself fifty dollars in cash and we could still live there."

The bartender set a couple more glasses of whiskey before Bud and Thomas. Both men looked quizzically at him and he pointed to the corner of the long room. Another coworker had set them up a round and toasted them with his beer. Bud turned and called, "Thank you there, Hank." Thomas raised a hand and nodded to the man and Bud resumed his story.

"A few years passed and here come a railroad right up our holler. A railroad, dammit! Up our holler. After that railroad come a couple of mines up the way. The railroad had took our big field, and Dad worked for a while clearing some of the woods but give it up before the next planting. Couldn't grow enough to get us by for the next year. That fall we moved to one of them houses at the minin' camp. I remember Ma was happy with that new board house. And it weren't too bad there. We had plenty to eat and the house was brand new. But we bought everything instead of growin' it ourselves. I was ten years old."

Now the barkeep set a couple fresh beers beside the whiskey and Thomas and Bud both laughed knowing they were going to end up drunk tonight. Thomas lifted his glass to Bud, who grinned and downed half his whiskey.

"Went on for a year or better and one day, I'd just got home from school and me and my little brothers and sisters was eatin' some pie that Ma had just made. Our neighbor come poundin' at our door. 'You better come quick,' he told Ma. She know'd what it was right off. Something had happened to Dad. Off she run with him and come back a while later crying her heart away. Got electrocuted by one of them overhead electric cables for the coal cars. Like them kind we make at the shop. Here I am going every day and makin' what killed my dad and what's sure to kill another bunch of folks." Bud downed the rest of his drink and sat staring ahead.

He studied himself in the mirror for a while then: "Well, we got him buried and all and was tryin' to figure out what we was gonna do. And here come the mine operator actin' real serious, just like he'd been ever since Dad got killed. 'Well,' he says. 'Have you found a place where you can go to live yet?' Ma cried, and he said it couldn't be no other way. Said all the men knew the risk of workin' in the mines. But Dad didn't see no risk when he sold his land rights. If he'd been able to read maybe he'd a seen some sort of risk with the whole business. After that it was too late to be thinking about risks. He had to feed the family, didn't he?"

Bud had gone red in the face and breathless at the memory and the telling of the story, and paused to drink some of his beer. He continued, "That mine operator said he'd let us stay there in the company house for another week. Ma thanked him like he was giving us somethin' real good."

"I shoulda killed him right there. They killed my Dad and turned us out of our house. Kicked us out the next week like we was a bunch of dogs. We didn't have nowhere to go, me and Ma and my little brothers and sisters."

Bud had to stop again and brushed a hand quickly past his right eye. Thomas looked at the gilt-edged mirror now and blinked his eyes at himself through the descending veil of alcohol. He knew Bud's story. It was the story of West Virginia, descended upon by liars and thieves who took everything and gave nothing.

"Finally come here to live. Ma went to work makin' up the beds at one of these railroad hotels. About a year later I found me a job and things was a little better for us."

"And now them son-of-a-bitches wonder why the miners are fightin'. Make out like they always done their part. I ain't a miner, but I'll be getting my licks in. Started carryin' a gun again. I'll be in it when I get the chance. I owe them people and I always pay my debts."

Thomas bought them another round and lifted his glass. "Here's to your dad."

Bud lifted his glass and drank the whiskey down. "Thank ya."

It was late when a man rushed in. "It's startin'," he shouted. "At Blair Mountain. Killed three men today, Chafin and his gang. Goin' to get to it now."

Bud lifted himself heavily away from his seat at the bar and slapped Thomas's shoulder. "Good talkin' to you, Greene. Sorry we took so long to get to know each other. I weren't raised that way. You know that, don't you?"

Thomas nodded, exhausted and drunk. "I surely do."

"I already been in one war for my country," Bud said, leaning on Thomas for support. "It didn't mean nothin' next to this one."

Chapter Ten

Thomas woke the next morning frustrated and hungover. He rose at 5:30, as he did every morning, and sat down to the breakfast that Gertrude had prepared for him.

She had been worried the night before, and had waited up for him until he staggered in the door at midnight. She hadn't often seen him drunk and it had hurt and upset her. But she didn't question him this morning as she sat across from him at the little oak table in the kitchen.

Thomas picked at the eggs and pork on his plate. He hated the thought of going to the factory and spending another twelve hours of his life standing before his machine, dodging the red-hot chips flying off the steel bars. "I'm sorry I didn't let you know I would be so late last night," he said. "We had to work until eight o'clock, and then I couldn't come home. We'll have to work late every day until we can fill a couple of new orders."

She looked at him closely. A dark oil smudge covered his right temple. He had not even taken the time to wash himself the night before. He looked tired … haggard, she suddenly thought. "It's done. Do you feel all right?"

"Well enough. I'm sick of my job. It'll pass, I guess."

He started eating, even though he wasn't hungry. He needed to eat or he would never make it through the day. In a few minutes he had finished and was on his way.

A dozen men were missing from the factory that morning, and rumors were rampant concerning the confrontation at Blair Mountain, where the marchers had been met by Chafin and his deputies. There were reported to be thousands of miners on one side and a couple thousand deputies and mine guards on the other.

Thomas felt on edge, like he should be doing something to help the struggling miners. As he began his morning's work, the confusion he felt was overwhelming. It just didn't feel right for him to be standing beside the machine he had grown to hate.

At lunch came more rumors from passersby about the skirmishing at Blair Mountain. Several more men were reported dead on both sides. The fighting was still going strong.

Thomas went back to work, though he still did not feel right. Something was seething, burning within. He was standing by the machine, staring at the chuck whirling around at 300 RPM's, when he heard the voice behind him.

"Them sons-of-bitches really did it this time," Pete Fawley said vehemently.

Thomas ignored him and went on working. "They were lucky to even have jobs. It beats all, these miners fighting the only folks who can give them work. We sure don't need none of them Reds in here telling folks how to run things."

Thomas turned and faced the man. "What do you think, Greene?" Fawley asked him.

"I think maybe you ought to live in a mine camp for a week. I think you ought to go dig coal, and see for yourself what's happening, instead of repeating what the newspapers have been printing."

Fawley looked at Thomas in surprise. "Anybody can make good if they want to," he said. "In this country a person can do anything he wants, but if he's going to be dragging his feet all the time and striking, he won't get anywhere. These unions are no damn good. They'll ruin industry."

Thomas stood looking at the man before him. He was like so many others, smug and stupid, with all the solutions to the problems in the coalfields.

"This is America. Hell, this factory is a good example of …. It took a lot of hard work to build this place into what it is now."

Thomas had heard enough. "You sorry son-of-a-bitch. You haven't done a day's work since you've been here."

Fawley's jaw dropped. He stared at Thomas in disbelief.

"I've listened to you blow off for long enough. I don't know why you come over here and talk to me in the first place. You talk about how fair things are. You may be right. It gives every man the right to become a crook. With a little luck and a lot of greed a man can join the rest of the crooks at the top of the heap. But not in the coalfields."

"A man can get something better if he cooperates," Fawley said angrily. "Why, I know these coal operators personally. I do business with them. They're good people. They've worked hard to get where they are."

"And where are they? What's the goal? Where's the opportunity for the man who has had his land stolen? Can he become a mine owner? Can he become what he has come to hate? Is he supposed to want to be rich and stupid like you, and live off the labors of men who can barely make enough to feed their families? If a man can't live as well in the mine as he did on the land, then he's got the right to destroy the mines."

Fawley stood before Thomas, his face reddening, amazed and angry at the outburst from this heretofore quiet man. Then Thomas was silent. What had been festering inside of him for so many days had finally come out. It could have been no other way for Thomas Greene. He would not listen to any more untruths. He was a man, a free man.

"You're one of them damn Communists!" Fawley cried. "You get out of here. You're fired."

Thomas set about gathering up his tools and other belongings at his machine. As he left the factory a short time later he felt good, like a tremendous load had been removed from him. He felt like laughing, running. But he had no job, a voice from within said! But another and louder voice pointed out that he was free. "Mountaineers are always free," a voice echoed through his mind. And a free man has the right to seek and tell the truth.

From the factory, Thomas carried his toolbox to the hardware store. They had sold him the machinist tools in the first place. Maybe they would take them on trade for a gun. That's what he needed, he knew, if he was going to join the miners at Blair Mountain. He wished he had kept his rifle, but Matthew had it on the farm.

He set the machinist's chest on the wood counter, and the clerk approached.

"Do you take tools on trade?" Thomas asked.

"Sometimes," the man said. He opened the box and looked over the assortment of micrometers, steel rules, tapes, and other measuring devices. "They seem to be in good shape," he finally said. "I'll give you half what they would cost new."

Thomas nodded in agreement, and looked over the display of handguns in the case below as the clerk figured the value of the various items. In a couple of minutes he had arrived at a figure. "New, they'd cost $118 including the tool box," he said. "I'll give you $60 for everything."

"How much is the forty-five," Thomas asked, pointing to the revolver below.

"That's $99."

"What've you got that will give me an even trade for the tools?"

The clerk pulled a boxed gun from the shelf behind him. He set it on the counter and opened it. "This is a .38 caliber. Just got these in the other day. The police are using 'em in the cities now. I got a good price on 'em. I'll let you have one of these even trade."

Thomas inspected the gun. It seemed heavy enough to do the job.

"Sold more guns this morning than I have in the last six months. Guess folks are getting ready in case that bunch of rabble comes down here."

"I'll take it. Give me a hundred rounds for it."

Thomas paid for the ammunition and set off for home. He was eager to be on his way. But as he neared his house, he began to think of Gertrude. She wouldn't want him to go. And what if he were killed, he asked himself. What would she do?

Gertrude was in the kitchen when he entered. She dropped her work and looked at him in surprise. "What are you doing home so early?"

"I lost my job. I told Fawley he was stupid. I've told you about him. How he comes around all the time asking me stupid questions. Today, I answered him, and he didn't like it too well. He fired me."

"Fired you?"

"Yes." Thomas sat down and laid the box on the table.

"What's that?"

He opened the box and lifted the revolver from it. "I'll need a knapsack and a couple days' of food. I can take the ham you cooked yesterday. That and some bread ought to do it."

"But … why? Where are you going?"

He looked down at the table. "I'll only be gone for a few days. I'm going to fight, to fight all the Hutches and Fawleys and Harrises in these mountains. A man's got to know what's right and wrong and stand up for what he believes."

Then Gertrude was crying. Thomas sat staring at her. How could he make her understand?

Richard entered the kitchen from the other room. His train had gotten into the Williamson yards at mid-morning. He stood beside the table, sleepy and bewildered.

When Gertrude stopped crying and Richard had learned of his father's plans, he told him what he had seen the night before. There were scores of deputies looking for men going to join the fighting. He didn't see how anyone could get through to the miners. A man by himself wouldn't stand a chance if he were spotted. Gradually Thomas was made to see that his plan was foolhardy.

"All right, I won't go," he finally said. "But we're going back to the farm. It's peaceful enough there now. And we can be close to Gabriel and Mary. That's my home. I'll not spend another day working in a factory, or for anyone but myself and those I want to work for."

Chapter Eleven

Return they did and resumed the life they had on their farm before William's accident many years before. They moved into their cabin, and Matthew and his wife, who had never had children, moved back with Gabriel and Mary.

The green had returned to the hillsides that had been stripped of their timber in former years. Time and nature had silently begun the process of salvaging what they could from the sections of the mountains that had not eroded to bare rock. The saplings that had survived the mining company onslaught had grown toward maturity. And once again, Thomas and Gertrude became a part of that which changes slowly and stoically, the land.

They were welcomed by their old friends and families. Of course Gabriel and Mary were still in the valley. And the Polands and Barkers were still there, as were old man Davis and his wife. The people Thomas and Gertrude had known had not changed much. They all had aged but time had treated them gently, it seemed to Thomas. Their lives had not changed so much, except as with Thomas and Gertrude, their children had grown and decided the paths they themselves would take. There was little difference from before in the lifestyle of the people of the valley; their source of life and food was still their land. And Thomas, as when he had first come to this valley so many years before, was contented with what he had for himself, as was Gertrude, who was happy to be back among her family.

The southern fields were still not unionized. The war at Blair Mountain had been thwarted by the intervention of federal troops, and the men had limped back to their mine camp homes to once again offer their lives to the mine companies.

Through the twenties, an exodus from the coalfields was occurring. Children were encouraged to make their ways beyond the dim opportunities that the mines offered. The mountain towns grew, and the industrial cities to the north swallowed the influx of mountain children without notice.

Then came the downfall of the coal industry as demand for the precious black stuff was diminished by the use of petroleum. The poverty of the mountains deepened and left people stranded. Mines closed and there was no work to be had. During this time and through the Great Depression, men and women often returned to their childhood homes to seek the security that a garden plot and a one-room cabin on the family homestead could give them. The abandoned mine camps with their crumbling gray shacks filled with men and their families who were out of work.

The Depression did not affect the people who had remained through the years, resisting the temptation to sell their land and move to the city or mine camps to seek the "better" way of life. As the outer world had developed technologically and economically with its assimilation of people displaced from their land, the mountain people had seemed in comparison to sink further into poverty. They never had much money. An economy of trade and barter had remained, and men worked at farming and the odd trades they knew to raise enough to pay their taxes and buy the few food staples they needed to sustain their lives.

In the spring of 1932, Gertrude had been sick with pneumonia for a month when Thomas sent letters to all their children telling them of her illness. But none of them could get free from their job and family routines right away to make the long journey to see their mother, except Richard, who was able to come because of his relative closeness.

When Gertrude died, Thomas immediately sent wires to all the children. That brought them. But by the time they were able to get to the farm, Thomas had already buried his wife.

"But why didn't you wait?" Mary demanded as they all sat in the cabin.

"It would have been nice to see her before you had the funeral," James said.

Violet was exasperated. "It's next to impossible to get here. You should have buried her in Huntington beside Robert."

"What you did is against the law anyway, Harold says," Mary told them. "You can't just bury a person anywhere you want."

"I wouldn't go by that law even if I knew about it," Thomas said. "That's stupid. This was her home. I've got the right to bury her here."

Mary and Violet and James had in the end blamed Thomas for their mother's death. "It never would have happened if you hadn't dragged her back to this desolate old farm," Mary said.

And Thomas knew that Mary was right. Gertrude might not have died in these same circumstances if they had stayed in Huntington or Williamson. But he knew that she was happy in their valley. Coming back to the farm might have shortened or lengthened her life. He could not tell, would not tempt himself with worrying over what fate might have brought in different circumstances. She was gone. He had loved her. She would still be nearby beneath the shadow of the mountain, and the pine tree he had transplanted over her grave would mark her place, mark death with life. She would be part of his land, his valley.

Gabriel was eighty-five when he died in 1935. Mary was eighty-one when she died the next year. Thomas mourned their passing as he had Gertrude's. But there was no lingering sadness in their deaths for him. Once they were gone and buried he set into his routine of life again, with the knowledge that death would one day release him from the world. He wished to be nowhere but where he was and to be no one but whom he was, and had no fear of being removed from it all by death.

Thomas made a simple will after Gertrude's death. He still had some savings from his city days, and this money and his land he would leave to his children. He made the request that he be buried beside his wife on the farm in a plain wood coffin. Thomas couldn't stand the thought of being forever encased in one of the heavy steel vaults used in the cities.

Even though he lived by himself, he was never lonely. He kept busy with the work around the farm, and at any time of the day or night he could seek out just about anyone in the valley if he felt like talking, or sharing a meal away from home.

In 1937 Thomas was seventy-seven years old. In summer of that year the strip miners came to his valley. They mounted their original attack on the mountain above the Davis land. Again came the continual dynamiting and the drone of heavy equipment.

Thomas stood watching them work one afternoon while talking to old man Davis, in his nineties now, but still able to get around. The bulldozers straddled the mountain ridge, pushing everything in their path over the mountainside. Whole trees were scattered down the hillside, caught in the undergrowth below. Boulders and huge chunks of sandstone were pushed over the edge.

"They can't do that," Thomas said to Davis.

"That's what I told 'em when they was startin'. Said to stay out of their way or they'd run over me. Said they got the right to get at the coal any way they need to. Cause of the mineral rights and all. Called it a broad deed or some such nonsense."

"It's not right."

"It ain't," Davis said softly.

A road for the trucks that would carry the coal off the mountain had been bulldozed up the long ridge that extended across Davis's land. They watched as a truck started down with its load of coal.

"They'll be above your land next year I s'pose," Davis told Thomas. "Feller said they owned the land or mineral rights for ten miles on the mountains along the river. They'll just keep going till the coal's gone."

"It'd be hard for one of those fellas to run over you if you had a gun."

Davis laughed. "I thought of that. They'd just put me in jail and I'd die somewhere away from here. I'm too old. They got me beat now. Long as one of them boulders don't make it all the way down here and flatten my house, I guess I'll be all right."

Through the winter the work went on. The highwall in the side of the mountain dwarfed the heavy equipment and the handful of men needed to run the operation. The trucks made their way from the strip of highway that led to Matewan to the dirt road that had been bulldozed along the railroad tracks. From there they crawled upward over the ridge on Davis's land onto the mountain itself.

From below, the activity seemed unreal to Thomas. What had taken time and nature millions of years to build took men a few short months to topple. Seeing the destruction of the mountains he had come to love hurt him. Once again he thought of the End that the Bible portrayed. The men in suits, the coal mines, and now this. He would sit and watch, feeling helpless as the trucks roared down off the mountain, the drivers racing to dump their coal and come back for more.

He was on his way to see Matthew one afternoon in February when a tremendous blast nearly pushed him to the ground. He turned to see its source and watched as an avalanche of stone and mud and felled trees careened and crashed their way down the mountain. A crushing pain suddenly seized his chest. He was forced to his knees and then lay on his back. There came a brightness through which everything was clear and vivid to him. Each tree that he saw towering above him was clearly etched against the gray, cloud-filled sky. The sounds of the forest lining the trail were amplified. Each detail was imprinted and recorded upon his mind. A peace settled over him as the pain subsided. He lay for some time in this state. A while later, as he felt himself returning to normal, and as he stood gazing toward the mountains, he realized that death might soon be upon him. What else could have given him the bright and lucid vision he had had? What else but death could have given him the peace he had felt?

He made his way slowly, ever so slowly because of weakness, back home and sat in his cabin for several hours, dazed and unable to think clearly. His heart was beating strangely fast, but by evening he felt strong enough to stoke the fire, though he was not hungry.

When he awoke in the morning before the hearth, where it had become his custom to sleep, he felt strong again. But there remained the vision of death. He would soon take his place in the earth. He envisioned the land he had come to love here in the valley as a child, and beside that mental picture rose the stark outline of the ravaged mountain that would soon backdrop his home.

He set his revolver and rifle on the table and loaded them. He considered how he would go about it, how he would confront the rapists when they reached his land. He decided that all he would need was the rifle. The revolver he packed away in the small box containing his important papers: the deed to his land, his will, and bank papers for his savings account. He bound the box with twine. On the lid he wrote "Important Papers." He set the box on the cupboard in plain sight.

And then it came in March. The bulldozers had been working the land behind the old mine camp. In a few short weeks they filled the gulleys separating the continuous mountain ridges, making it possible for them to pass onto the mountain behind his home. One of the dozers began rearranging the land that had once been his.

In the morning, he set off up the trail. Near the top of the mountain the trail was already blocked off with trees and rocks. He found a passable route after a few minutes and stood watching the dozer doing its work. It was a huge machine, unreal with its roaring engine propelling it on its destructive path.

Thomas levered a cartridge into the Winchester. All around him were trees and rocks and earth piled in unruly ridges, all to be wasted. The bulldozer approached, and Thomas shouted at the man operating it. But the roar of the machine drowned out his words.

Thomas waved his arms, holding the rifle in the air. The operator saw him and cut the power to an idle. The adrenalin pumped through Thomas's body. He could feel the pounding in his chest as he walked towards the machine.

As he neared the dozer, the operator sat calmly staring at him. He looked familiar to Thomas for some reason. The man on the machine craned his neck forward as if to see Thomas better.

The dozer man started to get down from the cushioned seat when Thomas was several yards away. Thomas leveled his rifle at him. "Just stay up there. You won't be needing to get off. Just turn that thing around and get out of here."

"Greene," the man called. "Always wondered what happened to you."

Thomas stared at the man before him on the dozer. "It's me. Bud Taylor," the other continued.

Bud Taylor. The years gave way to Thomas's memories.

"At the factory in Williamson."

Thomas lowered the rifle as he remembered the young man named Bud Taylor. "What are you doing up in these mountains?"

"Got to work. Got my leg shot up in twenty-one. Can't hardly walk on it. Got to feed my family."

"I'll shoot you if you don't get that thing out of here. This is my home."

"I'm sorry," Bud said. "But listen, if I have to back out of here, the law will be here right quick to get you. There's nothing to stop it. It's all legal."

Thomas raised the gun again. "You're not the Bud Taylor I knew. I don't know you." The thoughts raced through Thomas's mind. How? How could the man have changed so much? How could this be legal? How could men sacrifice their beliefs? How could he shoot anyone? How could he save his mountain? How could he make them understand? The End was supposed to be some sort of supernatural occurrence. This was black and white with scared men. How …?

The rifled dropped from Thomas's hands. The pounding in his chest became a fluttering. He tried to speak but couldn't move his mouth. No words could form on his lips. Thomas fell into the shiny clay that had been bared by the huge yellow dozer.

Chapter Twelve

"It's time to change him again," the voice came dimly through the darkness to Thomas.

"Let me finish in twenty-nine, and I'll be right with you," another called.

A rustling broke the stillness. The spring. The wind. Thomas's eyes opened, and he saw a white form bent over him. He felt the warmth of a washcloth as the figure lifted his legs and washed him. The figure seemed far away. Clouded. The light came to him through a thin, fuzzy veil. He was surrounded by a tent-like enclosure. Something hanging on his nose. A needle in his arm. Thomas tried to speak, to call out. Where am I? The thought echoed through his mind, but no words came. Where am I? He tried to sit up, but only lurched crazily to one side.

The figure in white stood up in surprise, then turned and ran from the place. In a few moments came a bustling entourage. The enclosure was lifted from around him. "Finish what you were doing," a deep voice commanded.

Thomas watched as a huge cotton rag was laid under him, and folded up over him to his waist. It was pinned in place.

"Mr. Greene," came the deep voice. "Can you hear me?"

Yes, he could hear him. He tried to answer, to say yes, but a strange grunt came out of him.

"Just lie still. Don't try to talk now. You've had a stroke, Mr. Greene. You won't be able to speak for a few days. Right now you're paralyzed. You're in a hospital. In Huntington. I understand you used to live here," the deep voice continued. "You're going to have to rest for a week or better before you even get out of that bed. Now I'm just going to check a couple of things and then leave you alone."

Leave him alone? Wasn't he already alone, encased in this shell that was his body? Hadn't he always been alone?

He felt his arm being lifted and wrapped in a canvas-like covering. Then came the wheezing of a pump. The doctor leaned over him. Listening through the stethoscope. He had bushy eyebrows.

"I've talked to your son in Louisville, Mr. Greene. He'll be here this afternoon. He said to be sure to tell you he was coming. You're doing very well," the doctor said as he turned to leave.

Doing very well? He wanted to tell the doctor he was already dead. A roaring filled his mind then. So loud. The dozer. Rocking back and forth. The mountain. No one there to protect it. The End. He felt dizzy.

Several faces took shape from somewhere. From years ago. One of them took his hand.

Another smoothed his hair back over his forehead. Yes. He knew them. Had they come to watch him as he died? Had his children come to him only in death?

"You're going to be all right," one of them said.

"Daddy, can you hear us?"

He stared blankly up at them. Violet began crying and rushed from the room.

Thomas tried to speak, to tell them that it didn't matter. James wiped the saliva from his father's chin with a white handkerchief.

One of them took a seat beside the bed as Thomas drifted off to sleep again, and the others left the room.

After Thomas had fallen on the mountain, Bud Taylor had come to his aid. He hoisted Thomas onto the dozer and took him off the mountain. By truck then, Thomas was taken to Matewan. And from there to Williamson and later Huntington.

And now on the second day his children were gathered to see him.

The others were confused over Thomas's condition until William got there later in the afternoon and saw his father himself. He explained to them that Thomas should regain full use of his body, and that speech would return within the week if he continued to improve.

William also explained to Thomas what had happened and assured him that all would be well.

The only cure for a stroke was time. The passing of
the next few months would return Thomas to his old
self, William told his father.

But Thomas felt only dread. There would be
no returning to his old self. There would be no place
in the world for him. A moroseness pervaded his
entire being. It made him sick to think, sicker yet to
feel what he thought. If only they had let him die, to
remain on his farm beside Gertrude.

A week passed, and he was able to turn
himself over in bed and control his bodily functions.
He had begun speaking even before the first week
was out, but did so only when necessary. He could
not stand to hear his words tumbling upon one
another, garbling his meanings. Like he was a baby,
the nurses would stop whatever they were doing and
peer into his expressionless face, coaxing him to
continue, to repeat what he had said until it came
out in an acceptable form.

The hope and strength he had always
possessed seemed gone forever and he expected
death any day. But the weeks passed, the sunshine
filtering through the second-story window of his
room. He watched, from where he laid, the reddish
buds forming on the maple trees of the hospital
grounds, and the silver-barked limbs taking on their
yearly adornment of thick-veined leaves. He
imagined his garden plot and the artesian well, the
smoke rising in a thin stream from his chimney in
winter, Gertrude's smile and love, and he willed his

morose feelings away. His decision was to go on living.

And then one morning came the news that he was well enough to go home. It had been decided by the children that he would go to Charleston to live with Mary and Harold. They had the most money and the most time to look after him.

Thomas left the hospital in his wheelchair on a sunny day. May 1 it was. He had been in the hospital nearly six weeks.

Thomas had never been in Charleston to see Mary and Harold, so his new home was a surprise to him. When Harold's Ford pulled into the driveway of an enormous home in the southern hills above the Kanawha River, Thomas viewed the place in wonderment.

Cut stone formed the exterior walls of the home. Mary immediately gave Thomas a wheelchair tour of the acreage. A brick path led around the side of the house to a rock garden in the rear.

"Maybe you can help me get my flowers growing better," she said to him. "They never want to come up very well. You were always so good at growing things," she smiled at the back of his head.

As Thomas gazed around the yard, and beyond to the woods, glimpsing other mansion-like structures along the paved, winding ribbon of street, he felt a sense of alarm—he was no longer in control of his life. And the realization scared him. Mary chatted on as Harold helped her get the wheelchair up the two stone steps at the back of the house.

"I just know you'll enjoy sitting in the yard," Mary continued. "We get squirrels and rabbits and raccoons. And one day one of the neighbors saw a deer."

Harold didn't say anything. Who was Harold, Thomas wondered. He had sold out his hardware distributorship the year before. Their children had gone their own ways. The last had left the year before. Two of them were living in Ohio, and the other had gone to Florida, where he had started a real estate investment firm.

It was hard for Thomas to propel the wheelchair through the thick carpet in the house. Mary helped him along and parked him in the corner of the living room by the fireplace.

"We'll have to see about getting some wood to build a fire for you," Mary said as she left the room.

Harold sat down opposite Thomas in an easy chair and picked up a newspaper. Thomas gazed around the room. The plaster walls were well adorned with pictures and other objects of art. Several chairs were placed in the room, forming a sort of circle. An elegant set of brass fireplace tools stood arranged in a metal stand before the unused fireplace.

Harold wrestled with the newspaper and came up with a double page. He got up and brought it to Thomas. "Thought maybe you'd like to read this," he said as he handed the sheet to him.

He searched the page for whatever article Harold had meant for him to read. Prices reduced on winter clothes. Entire stock must go. Ride in comfort and style in the all new Chevrolet. Tired of your home? Over fifty selections at all times. Thomas turned the paper over. At the top in bold black letters he read, "The Mountain Man Understood." First of a three-part series.

Much has been said and written concerning the people of the mountains, the "hillbillies" of West Virginia and the other Appalachian states. Myths have become popular through the prior decades of this century, myths that ignore the fundamental realities of the modern industrial state. It is time to lay to rest the untruths and misconceptions that have abounded to this time and that have portrayed the mountaineer as the inhabitant of the last frontier.

There is no longer the wilderness "frontier," the common usage of the term in this country for the last century. The new frontier has nothing to do with wilderness or with land of any kind for that matter.

We have witnessed the advent of the industrial society. And it is this society that has provided the new frontier for this country. One can no longer remain hidden away on a desolate mountainside and expect to share in the prosperity that this new frontier has to offer.

The mountain people cannot expect to share in this era of economic advancement until they realize that what is needed is not the continued isolation that has characterized their lives in an agrarian past, but the spirit of cooperation with the abundant industrial concerns of the mountains, and the realization that only these concerns can give them access to the prosperity of the new frontier.

One need only get off the beaten track to see that the well-publicized poverty of the typical mountain family is self induced. Only a week before this writing, this reporter was in Boone County to witness firsthand the appalling lack of community which is so characteristic of ....

Thomas put the paper down and looked across the room, but Harold was hidden behind his newspaper. He folded the paper carefully and dropped it on the floor beside his wheelchair.

"What did you think of it?" Harold asked a few minutes later.

"I was too tired to finish it." What did Harold want to hear? That the world revolved around hardware stores? That "hillbillies" needed to be understood?

Every morning at nine o'clock Harold went to play golf. "He needs the exercise," Mary told her wiry father. "The doctor said he should stay active."

And every morning Mary wheeled Thomas into the rock garden, where he would sit in the sun or practice walking with the aluminum-frame walker they had bought for him. His legs still felt clumsy, but each day he made progress. As soon as he regained full use of his body, he would go back to the farm. When he could take care of himself, no one would be able to stop him.

Thomas had been at his new home for eight days when Richard brought him the few things from the farm that Thomas had requested—some of his clothes and the box containing the deed to his land. But Mary would not give him the clothes. "They smell bad and they're all worn out," she said. He would have to continue to wear the shiny slacks and the colorful sweaters and starchy shirts that she had bought for him. He didn't fight it. It didn't matter what he wore.

Thomas questioned Richard about the strip mining. "They're way up on the mountain. They won't hurt anything up there," Richard said. But he evaded the other questions that his father asked and would not talk further of the farm. After a while, he went inside.

From where he sat in the rock garden, Thomas could hear Richard and Mary talking. But he was too far away to hear what they were saying. He picked up the walker from beside his chair and moved toward the open window.

"Can't stay there," he heard Richard say.

"What did William think?"

"That it will probably get worse. He said he looked at the results from the last blood test."

"What will happen?" Mary asked.

"He couldn't say for sure. Another stroke probably. Permanent paralysis, maybe."

"There's a good home. Not four miles from here. We'll wait and see."

Thomas leaned on the walker, then threw it aside. He didn't need the damn thing. He took several halting steps along the path through the garden toward his wheelchair. He was suddenly very tired. He had known all along. He had seen death, felt its peaceful embrace.

He sat in the chair again, thinking of his farm. He was separated from his land, the land that had always given him peace. How could he explain it to anyone? This feeling that something had gone wrong, that even now, as he sat in this idyllic garden with the bird bath and squirrels, it hurt him to know that the men and their giant machines were busily raping the mountains. That everything beyond the land and a man to work it was artificial. That industry and machinery and the money generated by them were not real, that they were just a passing stage in the ages of mankind, that they would someday topple over like the illusory house of cards they formed, that these things added up to the End.

The fear of losing control of himself, as he had with this stroke, seized him. He might go on forever, sitting in this chair, rotting in the halls of some old-folks' home, no longer in control of himself.

Richard and Mary came through the garden toward him. Richard stood before him, holding his suitcase. "I've got to catch my train," he said. "The taxi's already here."

Thomas stood up and the two embraced. "I'll be back in a week," Richard said. "I asked the trainmaster to schedule me as often as possible to Charleston so I can come to see you."

"Thanks for coming," Thomas said. "Give my love to your family. I would've liked to see them again."

Richard laughed. "You'll see them soon enough. In a few weeks I've got a vacation coming.

We want you to come stay with us a few days in Huntington."

Thomas watched as Richard walked around the house toward the street.

"I'd like to lie down for a while," Thomas told Mary. She pushed his chair to the steps and he stood up.

"You're getting better all the time!"

"It won't be long," Thomas said and stood smiling before her. "I can make it to my room. Would you mind getting my box of papers?"

"What box?"

"The one Richard brought. I want to look through some things before I go to sleep."

Richard got into the taxi. Then he was on his way down the steep, curving road to the broad valley below. He felt strangely as they neared the highway along the Kanawha River. What was it his father had said? *Give my love to your family. I'd like to see them again.* No. He had said … *I would've liked to see them.* Would've liked?

"I forgot something," Richard said to the driver. "I'll have to go back."

Up the hill the car strained, and in a few minutes they reached the house.

"Will you wait?" he asked the driver. "I don't know how long I'll be."

"Sure. The meter's runnin'."

Richard stood in the front yard. What was he going to say? That he was afraid that his father was dying, planning to die? Richard went slowly up the walk. He was almost to the front door when the shot reverberated within the stone house.

Chapter Thirteen

"But it's not a legal will," Mary said again. "Harold says that there has to be a witness. And besides, it's illegal to bury a person anywhere but in a cemetery. He should be buried in Huntington with Robert." Harold, sitting next to Mary, solemnly nodded in agreement.

"We can have Mother's remains dug up and brought to Huntington, too," James said.

"That would be best," Violet added.

"No!" William stood up, tapping his cane nervously on the floor. "You would betray his last wishes? No. I'll dig the grave if I have to. I'll take him down myself if you won't help."

"I'll help you," Richard said.

"But it's illegal," Mary said impatiently.

"Will it be illegal if the funeral home participates, if they take the body down?" William asked.

"I don't know," she stammered, and turned to Harold.

"A funeral home can't do such a thing either," Harold said.

"The hell!" William said. "Where's the phone?"

Mary pointed to the hallway.

William crossed the room and sat in the chair beside the phone. In the phone book he found the number of the funeral home where his father's body lay. "This is Dr. Greene," he said in a few moments. "Let me speak to the director, please."

William sat waiting. "It was horrible," he heard Mary say.

"I should have looked in the box. It felt awfully heavy," Richard said.

Then Harold was talking. "We've been over it all already. It's nobody's fault."

"Yes. Thomas Greene," William said. "He'll be buried in Mingo County. Yes, it's a change of plans. Hang the cost. No, it's a family plot." He paused and listened. "We'll pay you double your regular fee …. Yes, I'll take full responsibility."

By 10 am the next day, the procession was under way. By noon they were in Huntington. By two they had reached Williamson. After eating lunch at a small restaurant that Richard led them to, they were on their way again.

The road from Williamson to Matewan was full of chuckholes and covered with mud from coal trucks. Beyond Matewan, the main road was indistinguishable from the mud roads that fed onto it from hollows or railroad spur lines. It was evening when Richard directed the driver to turn off the highway onto the rutted road that had been constructed the year before for the coal trucks.

Then they traveled east on the road along the railroad tracks. In a few minutes Thomas's valley was in sight. As had often been the case since they had left Williamson behind several hours before, the tops of the mountains along the sides of the valley before them were bulldozed flat. For as far as they could see to the east there was nothing but destruction. The brown of the mountain ridges stretched lifelessly before them.

The hearse and the two black Cadillacs passed the mine camp. The cloud of dust trailing behind the cars concealed the old man who walked down to the road. Three times old man Davis fired his Winchester into the air.

The great cars passed the mine, and the road ended. From there they were able to slowly drive along the railroad tracks on the cinder right of way until they came to the wagon trail to the Greene farm and they parked.

"What was all the shooting?" Mary asked excitedly as the Greene family gathered around the hearse.

"I don't know," William answered, gazing up at the highwall carved along the top of the mountain. "But we better hurry if we're going to finish by dark."

"I don't like it here," Violet said.

"It's like we've never been here before," Mary said.

James and Richard and the drivers pulled the pine box from the open doors of the hearse. They started up the trail to the farm. "How far is it?" one of the drivers asked.

"Two hundred yards," William said.

They walked without speaking. As the Greene family traversed the wagon trail that bisected the unplowed fields of Thomas's farm and led to the cabin, Richard's youngest child tugged on the sleeve of his mother's dress. "Why are those people following us?"

Behind them, a group of people was walking toward them. William recognized old man Davis hobbling along at the head of them. They set the pine box down and watched as the ragged procession neared. A couple of men carried shovels. From above came another group led by Matthew Ransom.

"We'll be joining you, with your permission," Davis said to William.

William shook the old man's bony hand. "Please do."

The drivers from the funeral home stood to the side smoking as the people made their clumsy reintroductions after years of not seeing one another.

Then they were on their way up the slope again, approaching the mountain before them. Poland and Barker and their wives and several children stood waiting for them at the Greene cabin, which leaned crazily to one side. The people of the valley trudged silently behind the casket bearers and the Greene family. The chirping of the peeper toads drifted up to them from the river and echoed back from the mountain. A hawk's repetitive cry drifted over the ridge.

Several rocks lay to the sides of the cabin. A boulder rested inside the rear wall where it had stopped after its descent down the mountain. It had knocked the cabin from its foundation. All along the bottom of the mountain was the debris that had been pushed from the top. A couple of uprooted oaks, with crisp brown leaves that rattled with the breeze, lay near the artesian well, which still spilled its pure and precious water down its centuries-old spillway.

The pine tree with which Thomas had marked Gertrude's grave was now twelve feet tall. William pointed to the tree. "Over here." The men carrying the box followed him, stepping around the rocks strewn about.

Mary left Violet's side and walked toward the well. She returned with a small, whiskey-crock jug that was encrusted with dirt and mud. "I thought I saw something over there," she said as she chipped the dirt away from around the jug.

"Where did that come from?" Violet asked.

Mary stared up the ravaged mountainside. "I'll bet it was up there somewhere. It's a wonder it didn't get broken with all these rocks and everything coming down here. I'm going to take it home with me. You don't see jugs like this anymore."

The six men with shovels and mattocks had worked fast with darkness falling and leaned now on their shovels, sweaty and breathless. And then it was ready. They carried the pine box to the hole they had all helped dig and carefully lowered it to the bottom.

Poland stood beside William. "I'd like to say a prayer if I might," he said quietly.

William nodded.

Poland mumbled his prayer and turned away from the grave.

As the men shoveled the dirt over the coffin, and as the rhythmic chugging of the locomotives broke the stillness from afar, the tears came to Mary's eyes. She hugged the newly found jug to her breast. But she quickly recovered, brushed the dust from the front of her navy blue suit, and dabbed the tears from her eyes with a tiny, embroidered handkerchief.

Acknowledgements

Thanks to the following readers and encouragers: Amy Greene, Denton Loving, Rusty Barnes, Jacinda Townsend, Karen Craigo, Ryan Hardesty, Judith Ramsey Southard, Megan Fahey, and Jason Kaufman. Thanks to Orie Rush for cover art.

Biography

William Trent Pancoast is 67 years old and worked on **The Road to Matewan** for 45 years, beginning in 1972. Along the way he worked as a die maker and raised a family. He is now retired and lives in Ontario, Ohio.

Made in the USA
Charleston, SC
26 February 2017